# Chances Are

## A Last Chance Rescue Novel

Christy Reece

Published by Christy Reece
Copyright 2013 by Christy Reece
ISBN: 978-1484815403

# CHANCES ARE

She is his dream come true. He is her nightmare.

Angela Delvecchio has always dreamed of being an LCR field operative. As LCR's main researcher, she's helped rescue victims, but always from the sidelines. Until now. Last Chance Rescue has been asked to assist the authorities in apprehending a serial killer terrorizing London. Angela knows this is her time and her mission.

After the murder of his wife, Jake Mallory stopped believing in anything good. Now, as an operative for Last Chance Rescue, he's found a new purpose but he'll never let his guard down again. The beautiful and much too vulnerable Angela is a temptation like no other—one he dare not take. Hearing that she's going to be an operative is a surprise but Jake is stunned to learn her first assignment will be to bait and trap the Red Rose killer. Assigned to be her partner, Jake knows he wouldn't have it any other way. He failed the last woman he cared about…he won't fail Angela.

Angela thought going undercover as an exotic dancer would be the toughest part of the job and Jake thought keeping his hands off his partner would be his biggest challenge. They were both wrong. Taught to expect the unexpected, Angela faces events she never anticipated and Jake must allow the unthinkable. Now it's a fight for survival because evil has more than one face and to stay alive, death may be the only option.

# AUTHOR'S NOTE

Welcome to the world of LCR!

I am thrilled to be able to continue writing Last Chance Rescue books. Chances Are is a stand-alone novel, as are the previous books.

If you're new to the series, this book is a good introduction. You'll meet Noah McCall, the head of Last Chance Rescue, as well as a few LCR operatives. If you're already an LCR fan, I think you'll be happy to see some operatives from previous books show up.

Whether you're new to the series or a long time reader, I hope you'll be delighted with Angela and Jake's book. As you read, it's my hope you'll be intrigued by some of the operatives who haven't yet had their story told. And yes, that does include Aidan Thorne!

Happy Reading to all!

*This book is dedicated to my readers. You are the best!*

# PROLOGUE

*London, England*

He had been following her for days. She was young, beautiful, and deliciously unaware of anything outside her field of vision or interest. Without a doubt, she had no clue that her life was about to make a hairpin turn and dead-end abruptly.

It angered him that she was so careless and ill-informed. Did she not watch television news or read newspapers? How could she not know that the most horrific killer of the 21st century had invaded London? A modern day Jack the Ripper had paralyzed the city, bringing terror to every heart. Why didn't she know about him? How obtuse could she be?

Ordinarily he liked his ladies worldly and intelligent. Smart women provided that extra spark of excitement. A combination of skills, intellect, and beauty was a must. This one would provide barely any challenge whatsoever. And though beautiful, her physical attributes didn't fit his needs. Normally he wouldn't even consider her. So why this woman? He didn't yet know. Perhaps it was her complete disregard of his existence. It was as if she were deliberately snubbing him. He didn't take kindly to such ill manners. He was no one to be trifled with or taken for granted. She would pay for the insult.

Her routine rarely varied. She left her home at seven in the morning, stopped on the way for a coffee and pastry at Louie's Drive-thru and arrived at work at seven-thirty. The office she worked in was on the third floor. The light would come on at exactly seven thirty-three and he wouldn't see her again until noon. That was when she came out of the office and dashed across the street for her take-out deli. Five minutes later, she'd run back to her office and there she would stay until she left at six.

When she arrived home, which was only five blocks from her office, she would be there until morning. She had no visitors and received very little mail. At ten o'clock, she would turn off the mind-numbing television show she had been watching or put aside the book she had been reading, visit the bathroom one last time, and then be in bed by ten-fifteen at the latest.

She worked too many hours, ate unhealthy food, didn't get enough exercise, and spent too much time alone. Without a doubt, she needed a caretaker, someone who would work with her, shape and mold her, revealing her true potential.

When her time came to leave him, he would make sure he gave her a proper send-off. As she breathed her last breath, she would look up into his eyes and see his immense regard for her. In her last moments, she would know and acknowledge his greatness and be grateful he had chosen her.

# CHAPTER ONE

*Last Chance Rescue headquarters*

*Paris, France*

Angela Delvecchio sat at her desk and watched the world go by. As the pseudo-receptionist for the Last Chance Rescue organization, she figured she'd seen the entire world pass by her at least twice.

Years ago, she had come to LCR out of necessity. Her family had needed money. At seventeen, with almost no experience, her prospects had been few. The fact that Noah McCall had taken a chance on her still amazed her. She would always be grateful to him.

Some might call her efforts noble but she couldn't imagine making a different decision. Her family had needed her. Yes, there had been sacrifices. Instead of being able to go to university like many of her friends, she had taken night classes to obtain her degree. When all of her friends were partying and dating, she had been working or studying. She had no regrets. Helping her family hadn't come from nobility but from genuine love.

Last Chance Rescue had been her salvation back then and she couldn't imagine working anywhere else. The organization's philosophy of rescuing the innocent, no matter the cost, struck a deep chord within her. Only days after starting her job, she had realized her true calling. She wanted to be a field operative. The opportunity to be involved in a mission, physically assist with a rescue, called to her unlike anything else. She had known within the depths of her soul that being an LCR operative was what she was meant to be. Of course, that hadn't been possible. Putting herself at risk would have been selfish and foolhardy. Her recently disabled father had been in poor health; her mother's stroke the year before had made her health almost as precarious. Angela had to stay safe and healthy to care for her family.

But those years of doing the right thing were over and now meaningless. The family she had once held dear and protected ferociously was gone forever. A freak one-car accident on Rue de la Seine had taken them from her. In one fell swoop, she had lost her mother, father, sister, and brother.

Noah had told her more than once that Fate had a way of kicking you in the gut when you least expected it. How true those words were.

Over the years, her mother's health had improved, so much so that she had been able to take a part-time job at their church. Her father had found a teaching position that hadn't been too demanding. Max had been in his first year of university and Chloe was all set to graduate high school next year. And Angela had been breathing a little easier, seeing her loved ones thriving and happy once more. Life, at last, had been on the upswing for the entire Delvecchio family. Then that cruel bitch called Fate had swooped in and ripped Angela's heart right from her chest.

That had been six months ago and now she could feel herself coming back to life, released from the smothering sadness that had threatened to consume her. A few days ago, she'd woken with the knowledge that though she would give anything to have her family back, that wasn't possible. However, something else *was* possible. Something she had wanted for years. She could now pursue her dream of being a field operative.

Noah was more than aware of her dream. She had no secrets from him. From the moment she met the LCR leader, she'd felt a kinship to him as if they'd been related in another life. He had understood her desire to be an operative, as well as the reasons she couldn't pursue her dream. So he'd given her the next best thing—the full training of an operative along with the promise that if the opportunity ever presented itself, she would become one.

The image of a tall, dark-haired man came to her mind—a reminder that fulfilling her dream of being an operative wasn't the only thing that had brought her back to life. The moment she met Jake Mallory, her world had changed for the better. It seemed as though she'd been waiting for him all of her life.

When Jake arrived at LCR for his first day of training, Angela had been more than eager to meet him. Having done most of the research on his background, she already knew his strength of character, his heroism, and his pain. The moment she'd looked into his eyes she had seen an LCR operative.

Tall, even to her height of five-foot-ten, Jake was six-feet-five inches of gorgeous masculinity and hardness. His vivid blue eyes, chiseled jaw and swarthy complexion could make any woman drool. And he had the kind of world-weary toughness that said he'd been there, done that and hadn't been impressed. Yet, despite all he had been through, he had a gentleness about him. He also had a wickedly dry sense of humor that could make her laugh unexpectedly and a sexy, too-rare smile that made her toes curl. Jake Mallory epitomized every trait she desired in a mate.

Too bad Jake didn't feel the same way about her.

A sigh of hopeless longing exploded from her. What was the point in wishing for something that would never materialize?

Movement outside the window caught her attention. A middle-aged couple had slowed to a near stop in front of the building and was peering inside. With effortless ease, Angela went into her receptionist role. Propping her longs legs upon her desk to show off an almost indecent amount of smooth, creamy skin, Angela blew a giant bubble from her wad of gum and winked suggestively at the man. Startled expressions were followed by the couple picking up their pace and scurrying away. Mission accomplished.

She swallowed a small laugh. Some parts of this job never got old. Between her sparkly, skimpy attire, multiple tats and piercings, and ever-present mouthful of bubblegum, she had deterred more unwelcomed visitors than many border patrol stations.

Her eyes turned to the computer screen in front of her but her mind once again wandered to Jake. What would he think when he learned about her aspirations? Would that make a difference in how he looked at her?

Though she'd seen some measure of attraction in his eyes, he had never tried to take their relationship further than a back and forth light flirtation when he came into the office for an assignment. Angela, on the other hand, had done everything but proposition him to make sure he knew she was interested. Her efforts had produced zero results. It was enough to give a girl a complex.

She jerked herself out of her unhelpful introspection. She was who she was and made no apologies. As much as she wanted a relationship with Jake, he had no influence on her career choice. She was proud of the work she had accomplished for LCR. With her skills and abilities as a researcher, she knew she had saved lives. Still, she wanted more. She had the training and the opportunity…now she just needed the mission.

When she told Noah that she was ready to be a field operative, he hadn't seemed surprised. He had to have known it was coming. Being true to her nature, she hadn't waited for him to give her an assignment…she already knew which one she wanted and had presented her choice to Noah. To say he was shocked would be the world's biggest understatement. But the question remained: Would he agree?

There was a monster loose in London.

Noah McCall stared grimly down at the pictures before him. Graphic police photographs, depicting the horror of a gruesome murder, screamed up at him, telling him that this killer had no remorse, no conscience. Noah had seen hundreds of crime scene photos and many of them had turned his stomach. None had affected him like these. Something had to be done to stop the bastard. And he might have the solution.

Slumping back into his chair, he rubbed the crease in the middle of his forehead as his mind searched for another way. Assisting the police in apprehending criminals wasn't the norm for Last Chance Rescue but they'd done it on occasion.

Operating beneath the radar often meant not getting involved even when they wanted to intervene or assist. LCR enjoyed a good relationship with law enforcement officials and stepping on their toes was a sure way to ruin it. However, this time the officials had come to him and asked for help. LCR had the resources to go deep cover, for months if necessary. They also had something else—highly skilled and trained operatives who could hunt down this bastard and stop him. Therein lay his dilemma.

LCR's purpose was rescue. Each operative understood that victims came first and would risk their lives to save others. Noah's number one concern was the safety of his employees. His operatives were in danger every day but they usually knew the monsters they pursued—pedophiles, human traffickers, and kidnappers were scum of the earth but a somewhat known evil. This was a different kind of creature—like nothing they'd ever hunted before.

His people were the best trained in the business. They could and would trap this fiend and end his reign of terror. Noah's issues with this case came from one employee only. A trained operative who could kick butt with the best of them, shoot the whiskers off a cat without scaring it, and when necessary, lie better than anyone he'd ever known. But she had never worked an op in her life.

She had brought the case to him. With her knowledge of the inner workings of LCR, few things got past Angela. She knew they had been asked to help, she knew they had the expertise. And she wanted the op for herself. He had always known this day would come. He'd just never anticipated it would be on a case like this.

For years, Angela's family obligations had prevented him from assigning her any missions. She had been responsible for their welfare. All of that had changed. Her entire family was now gone and Angela's entire life had changed in an instant. One thing that hadn't changed was her desire to become a field operative. Truth was, when she had told him she was ready to be a full-fledged operative, he had been relieved. For months, he'd watched her frozen in grief, zombie-like and merely existing. There was light in her eyes once again. Damned if he wanted to douse their brightness.

With her skills, intelligence, and grit, he had every faith that Angela would be an excellent operative. What she lacked was experience. But was this the right assignment for her first time? A psycho-maniac who was abducting and torturing his victims before murdering them? This was a hell of an op to cut her teeth on.

The buzzer on his desk sounded. He sighed resignedly as he pressed the button. "Yes?"

"Can we talk about it?"

Her eagerness to get started was apparent. Hearing the excitement in her voice made him want to agree to anything just to keep it there. However, he refused to make a rash decision just because of that. "We can talk but I still haven't made up my mind."

"I'll be right there."

In spite of the grim nature of their upcoming discussion, Noah barked out a dry laugh. When she wanted something, Angela could talk a blue streak. He'd seen her wear down more than one person just by her sheer volume of words. Most of his operatives were taciturn at best. A dynamo with energy to spare, Angela could talk anyone into almost anything.

Her long-legged stride full of determination, she entered his office without knocking. Angela was one of LCR's most valuable assets and, other than Noah, knew the organization better than anyone. She had been in her late teens when she'd responded to his advertisement for a receptionist. As an upstart rescue company, Noah and his friend and business partner Milo Evans, had no clue on how to go about finding good help. Milo had often commented that the good Lord was looking out for them when he'd sent Angela their way. They had been looking for someone to answer phones and discourage unwelcomed visitors. What they had gotten was a computer genius with research skills not even the government could match.

Noah had liked Angela's energy and intelligence but most of all he had liked her loyalty to her loved ones. She had been determined to take on so much at such a young age and make it work. Even if she hadn't been a computer genius, he would have hired her.

There wasn't an LCR employee who didn't appreciate Angela's contributions. She made everyone's job a thousand times easier and had saved lives in the process.

She dropped down into the chair across from him. "So, what's your biggest concern?"

Noah had intimidated more men and women than he could remember, but to his knowledge, he had never done that with Angela. She had always acted as if they'd known each other since birth.

"My biggest concern is that you could get yourself killed."

"Since this guy is slicing and dicing his victims, that's a given. But whatever op I go on, something similar could happen."

"The creeps we go after aren't usually serial killers."

He knew better than to encourage her to take some time off and just enjoy life. That argument had already been made and lost. After all she had been through, one would think she'd want to spread her wings, maybe even explore life outside the confines of LCR. When he'd made that suggestion, he had been reminded once again of Angela's single-minded determination. When she wanted something, she went after it with everything within her. She wanted to be an active field operative. Now.

"There are plenty of other ops I can assign you. Dropping you into the deep end of the pool makes no sense. Only our most seasoned and experienced operatives should be on this case."

"I'm well aware that I don't have the experience, Noah. And I know which operatives you're assigning—remember, I saw your list. Eden, Shea, Sabrina and Riley are some of our best. But you trained me just like you trained them. I know what they know."

"There are some things you can't get in a training session. Real world experience is a hell of a teacher."

"So let me go out and get that experience."

Noah shook his head. "We're talking around the issue. I know you've got the skills, I just don't know if throwing you to the wolves your first time out is a good idea."

"Then assign someone to me who'll watch my back."

That was a no-brainer. If he put her on this op, he already knew who she would be paired with. A former military man and ex-Chicago cop, Jake Mallory had the discipline and drive that Noah looked for in an LCR operative. He also possessed the protective, kick-ass attitude of a seasoned professional. And with the bond Noah had seen growing between the two, he knew that Jake would battle the fires of hell for Angela.

Apparently under the impression he was considering which operative he could partner her with, she added, "Seth and Honor already know this case. Assign Seth to me. Or how about Dylan? He just came off an op and—"

Noah held up his hand. This was the price he paid for having Angela know almost as much as he did about the inner workings of LCR. Normally he enjoyed her input but this was one thing he would decide for himself. Seth Cavanaugh and Dylan Savage were excellent operatives but not right for this particular mission. "Finding you a partner won't be a problem. I'm just not sure—"

"Will you ever be absolutely sure, Noah? You've treated me like family from the moment I walked through LCR doors and I can't even begin to express how much that means to me. Without your generous salary, I'm not sure how my family would have survived. But that's in the past. Being an LCR operative is my future."

She leaned forward, her dark, velvet brown eyes searing his. "It comes down to this. I'm an LCR employee. And I'm a trained operative. This is an operation I know I can handle. It's time to let me be what you trained me to be."

Noah stared deep into her eyes for several seconds; Angela met his gaze, unflinchingly, unwavering in her determination and confidence. Finally, he took a breath and said, "Three conditions."

A brilliant light entered her eyes but she kept her expression serious. "Name them."

"No rash decisions. Your partner will be the experienced one. He tells you to do something, you damn well do it. No arguments."

She nodded. "Of course."

"You go through a two-day refresher course. Weapons, self-defense, and physical stamina. If your trainer says you're ready, you're ready. If he says no, then you sit this one out."

"No problem. And the third?"

Noah held back a grin at her easy agreement. Lack of confidence had never been one of Angela's weaknesses.

"I want you to talk with Samara. If she says you're mentally ready for the challenge, you're in."

"That's it?"

Noah nodded.

By nature, Angela was an exuberant, expressive person. Noah could tell it was taking every bit of her self-control not to get up and dance around the room. He had missed seeing that vivre. He just hoped to hell he had made the right decision. If anything happened to her, he would never forgive himself.

She settled back into her seat with apparent effort and asked calmly, "Who's my partner?"

His eyes eagle sharp to gauge her reaction, he answered, "Jake Mallory."

Multiple electric quivers zipped up Angela's spine. Maintaining as neutral an expression as possible, she held her breath to keep from gasping. She knew her boss all too well...he was waiting for a reaction. She refused to give an outward sign that her heartbeat had just skyrocketed. Noah was aware of her fascination with Jake. She hadn't exactly hidden it from anyone, even Jake.

Aware that he was waiting for a response, Angela nodded her approval and said calmly, "I'll be glad to work with Jake. He's extremely capable."

She wasn't fooling Noah. His slightly raised brow and little half crooked smile told her that. Okay, so what if she couldn't look at Jake without salivating or getting very heated in certain parts of her body. She was a professional and a mature woman. Her hormones didn't control her actions. Besides that, Jake had gone out of his way to show her he wasn't interested in her romantically.

Most operatives treated her like a kid sister. Their attitude had never bothered her before since she had always looked at LCR employees as extended family members. Until Jake. There was no way she could look at him and see anything other than a larger than life sexy man. One with all the necessary attributes and equipment to make her heart flip over and her hormones stand up and take notice.

Apparently deciding the meeting was over and the matter settled, Noah stood. Angela had no choice but to get up also. She didn't even bother to tell herself that her wobbling knees had nothing to do with the fact that soon, she and Jake would be alone together for hours, maybe days. But this was an op…her very first. No matter her partner, she would do her job to the best of her considerable ability.

"Send Jake up when he gets here."

Her unreliable, foolish heart skipped a beat. She hadn't seen Jake in days. Still, she didn't plan to stick around to hear what he thought about this assignment or his new partner. She would have to face him soon but not today. She needed to go home and regroup. Tomorrow she would be better equipped to deal with the fallout.

"He's not going to like it, is he?"

"It's not his job to like an assignment. He'll do what he has to do."

Not exactly encouraging words. Bad enough that Jake would be worried about her, but to have him forced to work with her wasn't going to be pleasant for either of them.

"Maybe you should assign me to someone else."

"All operatives on this case will have a partner." Noah paused a beat, and then with that adamant edge that meant he wouldn't back down, he added, "Jake is yours."

A hundred different emotions raced through Angela as she silently left the room. Setting aside her anxiety about Jake for the time being, she reveled in what lay ahead. She was getting what she had wanted almost from the moment she'd walked into a small, slightly shabby hotel room and met Noah and Milo for the first time.

After describing her qualifications, eagerness had lit up their faces like they'd just been handed their most wished-for Christmas present. Even then, her computer skills, mostly self-taught, were crazy mad.

A few months before he was killed, she'd had a conversation with Milo about this very thing. He had understood her need to do more but told her when the time came, she'd probably have to fight both he and Noah for the chance. Not because she was so good at research but because she meant so much to both of them.

Milo had been gone for almost four years now. An LCR operative turned traitor had sold them out. Milo had paid the price. Even now, it was still hard to deal with that loss. She knew that Noah missed him daily. Milo had been an inspiration to all who knew him.

The elevator landed on the first floor and Angela headed to her desk. She'd clear up a few things and be gone before Jake's meeting with Noah ended. She told herself she wasn't being a coward. She honestly did have a lot of things to do. It was just that when Jake found out, he would probably come looking for her. She had no problem holding her own with most people. Jake wasn't most people.

Falling in love with a man who only wanted to be your friend was a sure path to heartbreak. She was idealistic when it came to a lot of things but not this. If one didn't look beneath the surface, Angela knew she shocked people. But beneath the façade she wore for her job lay the soul of a true romantic. She wanted candlelight dinners, long walks in the park, and multiple orgasms. And she wanted forever. That wasn't anything Jake would ever offer her. Okay, maybe she could wear him down eventually to where he could provide the multiple orgasms. But she wanted much more than that. She wanted to be Jake Mallory's everything.

# Chapter Two

"Come on, sweetheart, you know you want it. Come and get it. I won't hurt you."

It had once been said that Jake Mallory's gruff whisper could charm the birds from a tree, the snarl off a grizzly and the panties from the most virtuous woman. He had never seen it happen but the talk had always made him laugh.

Today he was trying to do nothing more than charm a mouse from behind his fridge. Didn't seem fair to kill the poor thing but damned if he wanted to share an apartment with it. The cheese, an expensive Gruyere, had been a small sacrifice. Now if only the creature would cooperate.

His eyes scanned the miniscule kitchen with its two-eyed burner, coffee-stained sink and 1960s-style fridge. He needed to find a nicer place. The flat had been temporary digs to hang his clothes when he'd first moved to Paris. Working for Last Chance Rescue had seemed like the perfect job but he counted on nothing anymore. Everything in his life was on probation, especially the things that seemed too good to be true.

Working for LCR had panned out so far. He'd been an operative about four months now, been on a dozen or so rescues, saved lives, and helped put bad people away.

Nice to know that some things actually were what they seemed.

A year ago he hadn't trusted a soul. Betrayal and a boatload of guilt will do that to a man. And now, he trusted an entire organization. Working for LCR had restored his faith in people. Not all of them. Hell, he'd seen too much evil shit for that to happen. Even now, he stayed wary, just in case. Jake didn't trust easy. Never again.

His attention moved to the present as a tiny, whiskered face peeked out from behind the fridge. Holding his makeshift mousetrap in readiness, Jake stood statue still. A colander might seem like an odd device to catch a mouse but it was his best bet for a live capture and release. Giving up the cheap kitchen utensil was no problem, especially since he'd never used it.

The creature scurried to the cheese chunk lying in the floor. Jake waited till the twitching nose touched the cheese. Quick as a cat, he dropped the colander over the small heap, scooped up the now squiggling mouse and dropped it into a waiting shoebox.

Grabbing his keys and jacket, Jake tucked the shoebox under his arm and headed out the door. The abandoned building two blocks away seemed the perfect relocation and should offer plenty of company for the little guy.

The cellphone in his pocket played a familiar ring, telling him that his boss, Noah McCall, was calling. He pulled out the phone and held it to his ear. "Mallory."

"Can you come in?"

"Yeah. Half an hour okay?"

"Yes."

The line went dead before Jake could say anything else. Phone etiquette wasn't high on McCall's 'must do' list. Most of the phone conversations they'd had consisted of one or two sentences but the tone in his boss's voice sounded ominous and grim, more so than usual.

His head low to battle the icy, brutal wind, Jake strode to his car. Opening the door, he deposited the box on the front passenger seat and cranked the engine. As he pulled onto the street, he reflected on his boss. Before coming to Paris, Jake had thought Noah McCall was an urban legend. As a cop, he'd heard stories about LCR's successes but had dismissed most of them as someone's wishful thinking. It wasn't until he'd gotten caught up in the middle of an LCR undercover operation that he realized everything he'd heard was true.

Jake had been a typical tourist the day he'd met McCall. He'd been in Paris for two weeks, staying at hostels, roaming the streets, soaking up the atmosphere. He'd stopped in for a cold beer and a cheap meal at a not-so-high-class establishment. What he had gotten was a busted mouth, a black eye, and a job offer.

LCR had been running a sting. He hadn't known that. All he knew was two men were attempting to pull a young woman out of the bar and no one was stopping them. Jake had intervened and ruined the mission. Thankfully another sting had been set up a few days later that brought down a human trafficking operation.

Even though Jake had blown the op, McCall had been impressed with his intervention. Days later, the LCR leader had called and asked to speak with him. Though wary, Jake agreed to the meeting. And after listening intently, Jake's world seemed to right itself at last. For two years, he had been mired in bitterness and grief, with no real purpose other than to get as far away as he could from the life he'd once lived. McCall's offer had shown him a new path. Now he couldn't imagine doing anything else.

Making a quick stop at the abandoned warehouse, he unboxed his uninvited houseguest and watched it scurry away before he got back into his car. Not his usual kind of rescue, but what the hell. Killing something just because he could wasn't his way. If it had been, there'd be at least five less sons of bitches serving life sentences in Danville.

Twenty minutes later, Jake pulled into a parking lot five blocks from the LCR office. Probably could have gotten closer but he was counting on a long walk in the frigid air to keep his mind from wandering where he couldn't let it go. The moment he walked into the office, he would be greeted with what he told himself he shouldn't want and couldn't have. Maybe this new assignment would get him out of the city for a while. Lately that had been the only way to keep his hands off Angela Delvecchio.

The light-hearted flirting was becoming more than he could handle. The other day, she'd said something particularly provocative—damned if he could remember the words. All he remembered was how he had responded. He'd been within a half second of pulling her to him for a hot, deep, thorough kiss—an open-mouthed, tongue battle while their hands ripped at each other's clothes. She had been turned away from him and if not for McCall's voice on the intercom telling her to send Jake up, he would have gone for it—and most likely regretted it for the rest of his life.

Grateful that the freezing temperatures seemed to have stiffened his resolve, Jake pushed the door open. The instant he saw her beautiful face, every frozen part of his body was instantly heated. And the most frustrating thing was, Angela made no secret of her attraction to him. That kiss he'd been so tempted to give her the other day would have been reciprocated, of that Jake had no doubt. But what was also obvious was her innocence and vulnerability. Beneath that tough-girl persona, he'd seen the gentle, caring heart of Angela Delvecchio. A heart that could be crushed by some cruel bastard's uncaring selfishness. Damned if he would be that man.

Exotic dark eyes gleamed up at him. "Bonjour, Monsieur Sunshine."

Figuring he looked like an ominous thundercloud, Jake grimaced a smile. "Sorry. Need coffee. Spent my morning catching a mouse and haven't had any caffeine yet."

Her pretty nose scrunched up. "You need to find a nicer place to live."

"Can't argue with that."

"Deidre just made a fresh batch of coffee."

"Thanks. I'll grab a cup after I see McCall."

He could swear her eyes flickered with secrets at his comment. Which was damn odd—Angela was the most open person he'd ever known.

"Something wrong?" Jake asked.

Silky black hair swished around slender shoulders as she shook her head. "Have a good meeting. I'm running some errands, so I won't be back today. I'll be late tomorrow, too. And then I won't—"

Jake held up his hand to stop her. "I gotta get up to McCall's office. Let's talk later. Want to meet for coffee? Say around four?"

Her eyes went wide at the invitation but instead of agreeing, she gave another quick shake of her head. "No thanks, too much to do."

Before he could respond, she pressed a button to open the elevator for him. Another oddity. It was against protocol. All employees had to verify their identity by pressing a sensor key on the elevator. And usually she went out of her way to keep him talking for as long as possible. He told himself he wasn't bothered by her eagerness to get rid of him.

She turned her back to him. "See you later."

Frowning, Jake walked onto the elevator and waited impatiently as it shot to the tenth floor. What the hell did he think he was doing asking her for coffee anyway? That was going down a path he'd sworn he would avoid. Stupid didn't even begin to describe his rashness. For a man who wasn't known for impulse, that'd been a dumb-ass thing to do.

He'd done his best to keep their relationship on a friendly basis, but he was coming to the realization that it wasn't going to work. Being friends with someone you wanted to strip naked wasn't possible.

At that insane thought, arousal rose swift and urgent. Dammit, walking into McCall's office with a hard-on wasn't exactly a good idea. Gritting his teeth, he concentrated on everything but Angela.

The elevator door opened. Relieved that he'd been successful in dampening his desire, he strode to his boss's office. He'd table the self-castigation until after his meeting. Hopefully a new assignment would get him out of town, might even get him out of the country.

He knocked on McCall's door and then opened it at the gruff "Come in."

The LCR leader stood behind his desk, looking out the giant picture window. When Jake entered, he turned and nodded at one of the leather chairs in front of his desk. "Have a seat."

McCall wasn't known for his cheerfulness but the man's grim features seemed even more austere than usual.

"What's up?"

"You and Angela seem to have a good rapport."

Jake frowned. Where the hell had that come from? Mentally shrugging, he said, "Yes, I guess we do."

"She's still very vulnerable from the loss of her family."

His frown turned to a scowl. "I'm aware of that." That had been one of his main concerns when Angela made it known she would be open to something more than friendship between them. The last thing he wanted to do was hurt someone who'd already been hurt so much.

"She seems to think a lot of you."

Puzzled and getting slightly pissed, Jake said bluntly, "Want to tell me what the hell you're getting at, McCall?"

As if Jake hadn't spoken, the man continued, "Angela started working for LCR when she was seventeen years old. She's like family."

It'd been a long time since a father or brother had warned him away from corrupting a young woman, but from McCall's expression that was exactly what was about to happen.

"Not that it's any of your business," Jake growled, "but there's nothing going on between Angela and me."

"You're sure?"

"Hell yes, I'm sure. I think I'd know if there was. Did you call me in for an assignment or to dig into my personal life?"

"So if there's nothing going on between you two, you won't mind working with her."

Feeling like a dimwit, he said, "I haven't had any problems working with her."

"I mean on an op."

Jake's entire world shifted. "Angela? On an op? But she's a researcher."

"She's also a fully trained operative. She's asked for her first assignment and I've agreed."

His thoughts reeling, he tried to come up with a reasonable objection that didn't look like it was more than simple concern for a fellow co-worker. "She's had a tough time the last few months. You said yourself she's still vulnerable. You really think she's emotionally ready for an op?"

"She'll go through a mental eval, just like all operatives."

"But why put our best researcher at risk?"

"Angela's been training Deidre for the past few months. She's highly qualified and Angela believes she's ready to take over the researcher task full time."

Hell, he had no issues with Deidre. She was a sweet, middle-aged woman who had a tendency to mother everyone. She was also, reportedly, a whiz on the computer. What he had problems with was putting Angela in harm's way. His mind told him if she was a fully trained operative then she had every right to be out in the field, his gut said something different.

"Angela's wanted to be an operative since she came on board with LCR," McCall said. "We both agreed that her family came first. Since she was supporting them, she couldn't put herself at risk. Sadly, that's no longer an issue."

A heartbeat of a pause, then McCall raised a cool, questioning brow. "You have some objections?"

Yeah, he had some objections, but none of them were valid. Voicing the real reason for his concern was out of the question. Especially when he refused to pull at that particular thread himself. His shrug was deliberately casual. "Just surprised, that's all."

"I think you'll be impressed with her skills. I've asked her to complete a two-day refresher. Dylan will oversee it, but I'd like you to be there, too."

"Why?"

"Because you're going to be her partner on the op."

Hell, hell and double damn hell. So much for staying out of her way. Still, even as he cursed, he couldn't deny the relief. He would protect her. He had failed in protecting the last woman he cared for...he would not fail Angela.

McCall stood. "The other operatives will be here tomorrow afternoon. Be back here at three for the briefing."

Still feeling off-center, Jake got to his feet and followed McCall to the door. "How many are on the op?"

"Ten, including you and Angela."

He didn't know whether to be concerned with the size of the op or not. Having that many experienced operatives should ensure Angela's safety. "So what's the mission?"

"We've been asked by British authorities to assist in apprehending the Red Rose Killer."

Jake froze mid-stride. No way could he hide his reaction at the news. Angela was going to be working to capture a man who had been deemed one of England's most horrific murderers of the 21st century? A killer who had been referred to as a modern day Jack the Ripper. And the bastard liked only one kind of victim: Tall, beautiful brunettes...just like Angela Delvecchio.

*Shit!*

# Chapter Three

Anxious for the meeting to begin, Angela tapped her pen impatiently against the conference room table. As she waited, her gaze wandered around the room, touching on each operative assigned to this mission. She knew some of them almost as well as she had known her own family. Now they were her only family. Familiar grief clutched at her heart, causing a stabbing ache in her chest and a burn of tears behind her eyes. Taking slow, even breaths, Angela battled the pain.

Samara had told her it would be like that, perhaps for years to come. She'd be doing fine, carrying on with her life, and then it would hit her like a sledgehammer, making it all seem fresh and newly horrific. Her entire family was gone.

Losing her parents had been excruciatingly painful but in some ways easier than losing her brother and sister. Though her parents' health had improved significantly, they still hadn't been completely well. For years, Angela had lived with the knowledge that she could lose one or both of them at any time. She had learned to appreciate each day as it came.

Her sister and brother were different. They had just begun their lives—young, exuberant and full of life. She could become exasperated with either one of them and then they'd do something to make her laugh and she'd completely forget her aggravation. Having taken on so much responsibility at an early age, Angela often felt like a third parent. In some ways, she felt as though she'd not only lost her brother and sister but also her children.

A slender hand touched her shoulder affectionately. Angela pushed aside her grief and turned to the surreally beautiful woman next to her—Eden St. Claire.

"How are you holding up?"

Angela smiled her gratitude. "I'm better. Still have some rough days."

Eden smiled in sympathy, her soft gray eyes revealing an understanding and awareness few people could fathom. This woman knew all about loss and its aftermath. She had lived through her own hell.

"So do you know what the op is? Noah's been even more closed-mouth than usual."

Angela wasn't surprised. Not only had Noah struggled with whether LCR should take on this mission, she knew he had wrestled with the assignments. In the end, with the exception of Angela, he'd chosen some of his most experienced and lethal operatives.

"I can't say, other than to tell you to start looking for either a black wig or some expensive hair dye and lots of make-up."

Eyes dancing with excitement, Eden murmured, "Hmm. Sounds intriguing."

Physically, with the exception of her hair color, which was a lovely white-blonde, Eden fit the criteria that seemed to attract the killer. And she was as deadly as she was stunningly beautiful. If the killer chose to go after her, he would be in a world of hurt.

The handsome man sitting beside Eden, her husband Jordan Montgomery, was just as lethal. Not only that, if anyone looked at Eden the wrong way, Jordan had a tendency to get very upset. Angela had seen Eden become very amused by her husband's over-protectiveness.

At the sound of soft, husky laughter, Angela turned her gaze to LCR operatives Shea and Ethan Bishop, who were whispering to each other. Shea's eyes were bubbling with merriment as she smiled up at her husband. Ethan's face said something else. If they weren't in a roomful of people, Angela had a feeling that Shea would have been thoroughly kissed.

The auburn-haired Shea wasn't the killer's preferred type either, but with a disguise, she would blend in beautifully. Slender, with creamy skin and sparkling green eyes, she would attract any man's attention. And the fierce-looking Ethan would make sure anyone who came close enough to hurt his wife would answer to him.

One of the things Angela loved and admired about the married LCR operatives was their intense devotion to each other. They watched each other's back and trusted their spouse implicitly.

And though they weren't married or even romantically involved, soon she and Jake would be sharing a partnership where they would need to trust each other the same way. She already trusted Jake, but would he return that trust? Since this was her first op, would he doubt her abilities? She pulled back from her worry. No point in borrowing trouble or creating more doubts than she already had. They could and would work through any difficulties. She and Jake had a good relationship. He might see her as a friend and nothing more, but he liked and respected her. Once they started working this case, she would prove to him that she was just as capable as any other LCR operative.

A huff of exasperation caught her attention. Sabrina Fox, a vibrant redhead with the personality to match, was rolling her eyes and talking animatedly to the golden-haired man sitting beside her, Aidan Thorne. Of all the LCR operatives, Sabrina might well be the most lethal. A few months back, Angela had walked in on a training session in the LCR gym and watched in awe while Sabrina took on three men at once, all seasoned operatives. And then, unscathed and barely out of breath, the woman had laughingly walked away, leaving all three on their asses.

Sabrina was most often teamed with Aidan. Though there was speculation that the two were romantically involved, Angela knew that wasn't true. Sabrina talked about Aidan as if he were a slightly irritating but much-loved brother.

Angela turned her attention to Aidan and held back a dreamy sigh. There wasn't a heterosexual woman in this world who could look at Aidan Thorne and not feel something. Nicknamed 'the golden Adonis' by a few of the single LCR employees, Aidan could make the most married and committed woman's heart skip a few beats. Even as crazy as she was about Jake, she couldn't look at Aidan without appreciating the view. No mortal man should look that good. And if that wasn't enough, he had a great sense of humor and was a genuinely nice guy.

Tearing her eyes away from Aidan, Angela looked to the other end of the table where a quiet and pensive Riley Ingram sat unmoving, patiently waiting for the meeting to start. An unknown in every sense of the word, Riley had been an operative for almost two years and was the most mysterious LCR employee they'd ever had. She had read her file, done the necessary research for Noah to bring her in as an LCR operative and yet, Angela still felt she didn't know anything about her.

The man sitting beside Riley, and politely ignoring her, was Justin Kelly. He had been hired last year without Angela's knowledge, which was a rarity since she usually dug up every minutia of background on a prospective operative before Noah made the decision. It wasn't until after Justin was hired that she learned he was former military and had apparently encountered LCR years ago when he had been trying to rescue his kidnapped sister from a human trafficker. From all accounts, it hadn't been a good first meeting.

According to Noah, Justin was the one who had made the contact and requested an interview. She remembered that Noah had left for the meeting sure that the man intended retribution. Three hours later her boss had returned and said, "We've got a new employee, Justin Kelly. He'll start in a couple of weeks." And that had been that.

Since then, Justin and Riley had apparently developed a love-hate relationship. Angela had heard that they worked together better than many operatives who'd been together for years, seemingly able to read each other without words. Outside an op, they acted as if they didn't know the other existed. Angela found their dynamics fascinating.

Finally she allowed herself to focus on Jake, who was sitting beside Noah. Her boss had the usual grim, determined expression locked on his face. Jake looked equally forbidding. When his eyes shot to her, they seemed to pierce straight through. Angela's heart rate increased, thudding hard against her chest.

The instant Noah stood, the entire room went quiet and all eyes zeroed in on the LCR leader. "We've been asked, along with several other organizations, to lend a hand in the search for the killer who's been on a rampage in London for the last year or so—the one the press has named the Red Rose Killer.

"Here's what we know: All of the victims have been tall, attractive brunettes. The women are single, Caucasian…between the ages of twenty and thirty. His preferences are waitresses and strippers."

His eyes scanned the room. "We believe he stalks his victims to ensure that they live alone. Once that's determined, he somehow gets into their home and takes them. There's been no sign of forced entry in any of the victims' houses."

"Is there any evidence that he actually gets into the home? How do they know he doesn't take them at the door? Or somewhere else?" Shea asked.

"There's a possibility some have been abducted elsewhere but there have been signs of a struggle in some of the victims' homes. The theory is he gets inside, overpowers them, and then carries them out."

"How the hell have people not seen them taken?" Ethan asked. "At some point, you'd think someone would have noticed an unwilling woman being dragged from her home."

Noah shook his head. "Traces of Ketamine, Rohypnol and Scopolamine have been found in the victims' blood. Any of those drugs can render a person helpless without causing unconsciousness."

"And can make you do things you never thought possible," Shea muttered.

All eyes went to the operative who had been kidnapped by a madman several years ago. Shea had been given a cocktail of the very same drugs, had lost her memories and almost her life. Thankfully, Ethan had rescued her but the hellacious event had struck at the very core of their organization.

"Exactly," Noah said grimly. "Scopolamine in particular. It's been called the zombie drug for good reason. A victim remains conscious and will follow voice commands. When the drug wears off, the victim often has no recollection of what happened."

"I'm surprised there's any blood left to test," Riley said.

Noah nodded. "All the women have died from massive blood loss. Throats are slashed, severing the carotid artery." He looked down at a file in front of him. "It's also believed that once he abducts his victim, he keeps her alive for several days before he kills."

"Why do they think that?" Eden asked.

"A couple of reasons. Several of the victims have called into work or contacted friends and relatives informing them they were going to be gone for a few days. When they didn't come back to work or reappear, relatives and friends went to check. The homes were empty. Mail and paper stacked up—indicating the women have been gone for a while.

"Also, the amount of torture he's inflicting would take hours, if not days. It's believed he keeps them between three and eight days. His torture methods are as varied as they are horrific. Electrical shock, strangulation, and burning their skin are just a few of them. After he kills each victim, he dresses them and then dumps the bodies in high-traffic areas around London."

"Sounds like he wants to get as much press exposure as he can get," Jake said.

"Yes, and the press has been more than happy to oblige," Noah said.

Pulling photographs from a thick folder, Noah passed them to Jake. Angela had already seen a couple of the photographs. Beautiful women, dressed in elegant evening gowns, hair and makeup in perfect order, and a single red rose clutched in their hands. The only thing that marred their pale, lifeless beauty was the hideous gaping slash across their throats. The evening gown covered the multitude of torture marks on their skin.

Jake examined the photographs, passed them to his left and lifted his gaze to Angela. She saw questions, concern, and not a little bit of anger. The anger was justified. She should have been brave enough to talk to him yesterday. Bravery wasn't usually an issue for her. She had no doubts about her courage but Jake brought out a unique vulnerability in her. She wanted to please him.

"How many victims?" Shea asked.

"Ten that we know of. At first it was one murder every three or fourth months. For the past two months, it's been one about every eight to ten days."

"His need is increasing," Jordan said grimly. "Do we know whether he already has another victim picked out before he kills his current victim?"

Noah shook his head. "No, and that's just one of the many things we don't know. Maybe he targets several. That way, as soon as he's done with one, he already has another lined up. But from the amount of torture he's inflicting on these women, he's spending a considerable amount of time with them. It'd be hard for him to commit a lot of hours to stalking."

"Other than their occupations, does anything else link the victims together?" Sabrina asked.

"Not as far as we know. However, there are four areas of the city he seems to be concentrating on. You'll see your assignment is in one of these areas.

"British authorities called me in for a consult the day they found their fifth victim. Honor, Seth and I flew to London and met with them. I offered LCR's assistance at that time but it was refused. The day they found the eighth victim, they called, asking for our help."

Angela remembered the day they returned. All three had the same bleak, sad look on their faces. Seth Cavanaugh had been a cop and his wife Honor was a former FBI agent. Both had seen their share of evil things. Angela had immediately known this wasn't the average killer. This man was a monster. One that had to be stopped.

"There's one more distinguishing factor," Noah said. "Each woman received a bouquet of red roses the day before she was attacked."

Shea nodded. "So that's where the press came up with the Red Rose Killer. I haven't seen any mention of the single rose found in the victims' hands."

"Right," Noah confirmed. "That's one of the few things they've been able to keep from reporters."

"What about florist shops?" Sabrina asked. "Any idea where he's buying the flowers?"

"No. There are no cards indicating which florist made the arrangement. It's assumed he buys them from all over the city. Probably pays cash. There are thousands of rose bouquets purchased every day. It'd be damn hard to trace every one of them." Noah lifted his shoulders in a shrug, his dark expression showing his frustrations with the lack of knowledge. "Hell, we're not even sure how the flowers get delivered."

"Could be that's how he's getting inside," Justin said.

Noah nodded. "That's why the news outlets released the information about the roses. Even though it pissed off the entire flower industry, women need to be aware that he may be posing as a flower delivery person."

In her usual direct way, Riley said, "So what's the plan? How are we going to trap him?"

Noah stood and pulled down a map of London attached to the wall. "With ten of you and four targeted sections, we're going to put two teams in one section and one each in the other three sections. You'll make yourself as approachable and visible as possible but not so much that he suspects you're anything other than a possible victim."

"So this is basically a fishing expedition," Aidan said.

"Right now, all we can do is fish. Bait the hook with what he desires most and then hopefully catch him."

"And if he does take another victim before he kills the one he already has?" Shea asked.

If possible, Noah's expression became grimmer. "Unfortunately, it may come down to allowing an abduction to take place. We'll have to wait and see. If he takes the bait and we believe he still has a victim…" He shrugged. "The scenario will have to remain fluid. You'll be issued jewelry with tracers in them. If you have to be taken, we'll track and find you. And hopefully save another victim."

Hands pressed against the table, Noah leaned forward and targeted each female operative with a hard, telling look. "That does not mean putting yourself in dire danger. If it comes down to a fight for survival, you take the bastard down, without hesitation. Understand?"

The room went strangely silent as if everyone was absorbing the gravity of the upcoming mission.

Angela felt Eden stiffen beside her. "I'm assuming we're doing our usual pairing off but where's Jake's partner?"

If she had expected Noah to announce that Angela was now a field operative or Jake to proudly proclaim that she was his partner, she would have been sorely disappointed. Both men looked pointedly at her, waiting for her to make the announcement. That was fine with her. Though she had proven her worth numerous times with intel and obscure information it might take someone years to uncover, she had yet to prove herself in the field. But, as she did with everything else in her life, she was eager for the challenge.

Determined to sound casually professional as if it was a foregone conclusion, Angela put just the right amount of confidence in her tone as she announced, "I'm Jake's partner."

Shocked silence followed and then the room exploded with protests.

Jake took in everyone's reaction. The other operatives were going through what he had felt when he heard the news—shock and disbelief. But no matter his concerns, which he couldn't say were without prejudice, McCall had faith in Angela's abilities. The LCR leader would never put Angela at risk if he didn't think she could handle the mission.

As the operatives stated their objections, Jake watched Angela. When she announced that she was to be on the op, her voice had been filled with confidence and pride. Now, as the protests continued, he could see that self-assurance quickly eroding. Though he knew everyone's opposition came from concern and affection for Angela, he didn't like seeing her confidence shattered. She would have to prove herself like any other operative but as far as he knew, not one of them had endured this type of trial before they went on a mission.

Jake surged to his feet, immediately catching everyone's attention. Using the commanding tone he had perfected in the Army, he said, "Angela is a highly trained LCR operative. McCall put her on the case because he knew she could handle it." He dug deep and added, "I'm happy to be working with her."

He glanced over at McCall, whose face remained impassive but Jake saw an approving gleam in his dark eyes. No doubt this was what the man had been waiting for. If McCall had announced his support first, it would have weakened Jake's own claim.

Angela's expression was the one that worried him. She looked as though he'd just awarded her a coveted prize. He didn't regret voicing his support but that didn't mean they weren't going to have a long, serious talk. Revealing his concerns to the rest of the team would serve no purpose. But as his partner, she needed to know where he stood.

Eden and Shea seemed to be the most disturbed by the news.

"I have no question that she can do anything she sets her mind to." Eden turned to Angela. "Don't for a second think I doubt your abilities. I just…" She paused for a second and added, "It's just...this isn't our normal type of rescue."

"I agree," Shea added. "I know you're as trained as anyone, Angela, but you've been through so much the last few months. Wouldn't it be better to wait for another, less dangerous mission your first time out?"

Jake took his seat again, waiting to see how Angela would handle herself. How she reacted would give him a good indication of how she would handle his issues.

Though her smile trembled slightly, he was glad to see a glint of determination. "With the exception of Noah, I've been with LCR longer than any of you. I'm more than aware this isn't the normal type rescue but that doesn't mean the elements are all that different. This is an undercover op. We're going to bait and trap this guy, rescue anyone we can, and stop him from killing again. The crimes might be more gruesome than the typical human trafficker or kidnapper, but evil is evil."

Before either woman could respond, Noah spoke, "Well said, Angela." His gaze swept the room, meeting each operative's eyes, one by one, as he continued, "Angela Delvecchio is a full-fledged LCR field operative. Every one of you had a first mission. This is Angela's. I expect you to give her your full support."

Not one to back down, Eden's eyebrows arched as she said, "I think I can speak for Shea, too, and say that Angela has our full support, Noah. That doesn't discount our concern." She turned to Angela again. "You're the little sister I never had. Of course I'm going to be worried about you."

Angela's smile was so breathtaking, Jake's heart flipped at its brilliance. And he was going to be her partner? Possibly for weeks? He saw a lot of sleepless nights and cold showers in his future.

"All of you know how important you are to me," Angela said. "LCR is my family. But I've wanted to be a field operative for as long as I've worked here. I couldn't." She cleared her throat, as her eyes darkened with a deep sadness Jake knew would be with her for years. "Now I can. I don't want to wait any longer."

Before any more objections could be made, McCall announced, "Ingram and Kelly will be in the same section with Angela and Mallory."

McCall hadn't mentioned this yesterday but it didn't matter. Jake approved. Angela's first assignment was a hell of a lot more dangerous than what most new operatives would have their first time out. McCall was making sure she had additional protection. Keeping Angela safe was priority number one.

Instead of protesting that she didn't need extra protection, Angela nodded and flashed an approving smile to both Ingram and Kelly. "Sounds great."

The tension in the room eased slightly. Recognizing that the discussion could move forward, McCall stood and began a slow walk around the table, passing out folders. "Here are the details of your assigned area and undercover identities. We've developed covers for you at your place of employment, as well as your apartment buildings. Only the upper management of your employer is aware of who you are."

He gave them time to open their folder and do a quick check of their cover profile. Jake briefly perused his undercover identity and nodded. Sounded easy enough to carry out. Flipping to the next page, he glanced at Angela's cover. His breath caught in his throat. What the hell?

Lifting his eyes, his gaze shot straight to his new partner. She was the one who set up most of LCR's covers. He saw the challenge in her eyes, confirming his thoughts. She had known he would have problems with her cover.

Angela, a stripper? Hell yeah, he had a problem with that. A major problem.

# CHAPTER FOUR

Angela gathered her assignment folder and stood. As the operatives left the room, each stopped briefly to show support, either by giving her encouraging words or a pat on the back. That meant so much. And even though Eden and Shea had voiced objections, she had no worries. Their opposition came from concern and caring, not lack of faith. They'd been like sisters to her. Her only concern now was the dark, brooding man in the corner.

"I think someone's wanting a chat with you," Eden murmured.

A shiver she couldn't hide zipped up her spine. Eden, Shea and Sabrina all gave her encouraging smiles and walked toward the door. Surprising the hell out of her, Riley stood close to Angela and said, "Want me to stay here with you?"

She and the other woman had probably exchanged only a couple of dozen words since Riley had started with LCR. The young operative said hello when she came in for her assignments and goodbye when she left. For her to act so protective touched Angela. Most LCR people were that way by nature, but for some reason, she felt there was another cause for Riley's concern.

Whatever the reason, Angela knew she needed to handle Jake on her own. She wasn't looking forward to their first argument. He had expressed support for her but would that continue in private? Would he try to talk her out of this? She wouldn't pull out of the op, but when he'd voiced his support, the feeling had been extraordinary. Of course she wasn't naïve enough to believe he was totally onboard yet, but she had every intention of convincing him of her skills and abilities. Someday soon she hoped he would completely believe the words he'd spoken.

She smiled her gratitude for Riley's offer and shook her head. "Thanks, but I'll be fine. He looks vicious but he's mostly bark."

Shooting Jake a fierce, warning look, Riley turned back to Angela. "Looks can be deceiving."

Though a bit indignant on Jake's behalf, Angela couldn't help but be pleased to see a different side of the mysterious, much too solemn operative.

Riley walked out, leaving only Noah and Jake with Angela. Surprisingly, Noah gave Jake the same kind of look Riley had just given him. Only Noah's had more teeth. She was glad her boss had never looked at her that way.

As Noah passed her, he said, "Samara is expecting you Thursday at two."

Angela nodded her thanks. She had no worries about talking to Samara. They talked almost daily anyway. Even though this wasn't their usual friendly get-together, there were no major secrets to be revealed. She might work for an organization filled with classified information but inside LCR, Angela had, with the exception of a few minor issues, been an open book. Besides, Samara McCall was one of her best friends—there was nothing she didn't know about Angela.

The upcoming physical stamina tests with Dylan concerned her even less. She was in excellent shape. Grief might have softened the edges of her mental toughness but her daily runs and hours at the gym had helped keep her sane. She knew she could do this job. Convincing Samara or Dylan of her readiness wasn't a concern. No, her biggest worry was the man who stared at her as if torn between yelling obscenities and spanking her.

She chose to attack first. "I can do this job so don't try to talk me out of it."

Instead of answering immediately, he walked toward her, his steps slow and determined, like a wild animal stalking his prey. Angela swallowed hard but stood her ground, waiting for him to reach her.

With only inches to spare, he stopped in front of her, and in a voice that rumbled like soft thunder, said, "Did I say you couldn't do this job?"

"No, but you—" She stopped abruptly. Okay, so maybe she should have waited to see what he had to say.

"But I, what? Am I concerned for you? Hell, yeah. Do I wish you'd wait until a less dangerous assignment came along for your first time out? Double hell yeah. What I'd most like to know is why you didn't tell me yourself?"

"Noah only approved it yesterday. You know missions can't be discussed until he officially takes them on."

Though she was telling the truth, she couldn't help but feel guilty. She'd had the opportunity to talk to him yesterday and had run away from it. She wasn't proud of her lack of courage.

"Fine. I'll give you that. But why didn't you ever mention you wanted to be a field operative?"

Considering she'd told him almost everything else about herself, she could understand his bewilderment. Tilting her head, she said, "What would you have said if I'd told you?"

His eyes seared her for several seconds and then he gave an explosive sigh. "I would have tried to talk you out of it."

She smiled her appreciation of his honesty. "That's what I thought. I've wanted to be a field operative for years. I couldn't because my family depended upon me." Drawing in a shaky breath because the pain was still so massive, she added, "I don't have that anymore."

Compassion flashed in his eyes. "You have plenty of people depending on you to stay safe." He drew closer, the sympathetic look gone in an instant, replaced by a steely directness she wasn't used to seeing. "Understand one thing. Our friendship cannot get in the way of this op. You do something stupid, don't expect me to be easy on you. I'll haul your ass off the job, if necessary."

Her feet were moving before she realized it. Closing the distance between them, Angela could feel the heat of his body, smell the musk of his aftershave. "Friendship?" she challenged softly. "Is that what we have?"

Desire flared like a rocket in his eyes. She had seen evidence of attraction but nothing like this. Before she could glory in that look, he shut it down, his expression going impassive and cool. Though he was mere inches from her, she felt the distance as if it were a thousand miles.

"Yes, friends." He paused and then added with humiliating emphasis, "And nothing more."

The hurt came swift, slashing like a knife against her vulnerable heart. Angela shoved it away, refusing to get sucked into the pain. Jake might be attracted to her, but he didn't want to have a romantic relationship with her. That was no different than what she had already known. Nothing had changed. End of story.

Jake felt like the lowest of slugs. That hadn't been the most diplomatic way to tell her there could be nothing between them. Still, it was for the best. After the trauma Angela had been through, she didn't need to get involved with a battle-scarred jerk who'd seen too much hell to ever believe in fairy tales and promises of forever.

Her smile obviously forced, she took several steps away from him and nodded stiffly. "Thanks for setting the record straight. I won't embarrass myself again."

"Angela, dammit..."

"Don't worry about it, Jake." Turning her back to him, she threw over her shoulder, "I've got two days of evals with Dylan and then a meeting with Samara on Thursday. I guess I'll see you Friday so we can discuss the case."

"I'll be at the evals with Dylan."

That stopped her in her tracks. She turned around to glare at him. Those beautiful, chocolate brown eyes that had looked so sad and defeated a few second ago were shooting brilliant sparks of temper. "Why do you have to be there?"

Fighting a grin at her quick temper, he made sure his tone told her there was no room for arguing this point. "We're partners on this case. Wherever you go, so do I. Besides, I need to know your limits and your weaknesses."

She turned her back to him again and snapped, "Fine. I'll see you tomorrow."

As she walked out of the room, her shoulders so stiff they looked as though they could crack, he couldn't help but let his eyes sweep over her. She was just so damned beautiful.

Jake had never considered himself to have a type before. Over the years, many women, with different looks and shapes, had attracted him. He was thirty-five years old and had been noticing and appreciating women for a long time. His wife, Teresa, had been slender, medium height, with brownish-blonde hair. He had thought she was one of the most attractive women he'd ever known. But Angela was… He sighed and rubbed the back of his neck where a knot of tension had developed. Angela was unlike any other woman. It wasn't just her exotic, sultry beauty that attracted him, it was a thousand other things, too. She had spirit, determination and drive, along with a vitality that radiated a love of life. And her loyalty and love for her family had been remarkable. She had put their needs before her own desires. That not only took enormous discipline but a tender, giving heart.

Now that caring for them was no longer part of her life, it only made sense that she would want to fill that void. Staying occupied helped with grief, he knew that all too well. But dammit all to hell, why did putting her life at risk have to be included?

He rubbed the back of his neck again, something he figured he'd be doing a lot over the next few weeks. Whatever Angela's reasons, it was a done deal and was going to happen whether he liked it or not. Best thing he could do was make sure she was adequately equipped to handle whatever came her way.

They were hunting a remorseless killer, something, as far as Jake knew, LCR had never done before. As a cop, he'd seen more than his share of evil people and had apprehended quite a few. Two he had shot to death.

This assignment would be the toughest he'd ever had for a whole different reason. Finding a serial killer would be hard enough and keeping Angela safe would be priority one. However, he had a feeling one of his biggest challenges would be keeping her at arms length.

# CHAPTER FIVE

*LCR Training Facility*

*Paris*

Hands on her knees, Angela stayed low as she concentrated on pulling air evenly through her lungs, then exhaling slowly. She had to focus. Jake's presence wasn't the least bit helpful. For every assignment Dylan had given her, she had known Jake was on the sidelines, his eyes sharply assessing…judging. She was in excellent shape, but so far, she'd probably given both men serious doubts that she could handle this mission.

"You okay?" Dylan asked.

"I'm fine," she snapped.

"He's only being tough on you to save your life."

In an instant, Angela straightened and turned to glare at the non-sweating, gorgeous man a few feet away. Jake's condescending words were infuriating. Knowing she smelled like a dead skunk certainly didn't help. "I don't expect him to take it easy on me. I don't need easy."

"Then what's your problem?"

Shouting that he was the problem would get her thrown out of this mission and rightly so. If she couldn't handle Jake staring at her, how was she going to strip down to almost nothing in front of a crowd of strangers, many of them ogling her and making all sorts of sexually explicit comments? She'd always had the kind of confidence to carry on no matter what was happening around her. The opinions of others had never really fazed her, mostly because she was sure of herself and her abilities. She knew who she was. But this was different. She had to prove to Dylan that she was capable and could do this job. And she had to prove it to her partner, too. It couldn't matter that her partner was also the man she fantasized about every night. She had waited years for this opportunity. Her libido would not stop her from fulfilling her dream.

"It's just taking me a while to get into the swing of things. I'll be fine."

"The killer isn't going to wait for you to 'get into the swing of things.' "

Jake's sarcasm was not only unappreciated, he used his fingers to make quotations of her words. She hated when people did that.

Whirling around, Angela faced Dylan again, who'd stood watching and waiting silently as she and Jake argued. The gleam in his green eyes told her he knew she was pissed; the slight smile on his face told her he was pleased. Realization came quick. They had played her and she'd fallen for it. She mentally shrugged. It had worked. They were all in this together. This wasn't some arbitrary test set up to anger her or destroy her confidence. This was a test most operatives had to complete...she was no different.

Now to show them what she was really made of. Focused on her target, Angela went after her opponent with everything she had.

Dylan blocked every punch she threw. Angela hit hard and low, surprising him with a punch to his gut. She barely got the chance to appreciate his huff of air before he grabbed her arm, whirled her around and threw her to the mat.

Back on her feet in an instant, she warily watched Dylan circle her. The man on the sidelines no longer existed. This was a fight for survival. It was she or Dylan. He struck again, this time coming at her with what looked like a knife. She kicked the weapon from his hand, grabbed his forearms to jerk him around and slammed him face-first onto the mat. Jumping on top of him, she grabbed his left arm and twisted it behind his back. "Gotcha."

Laughter burst from Dylan; the man watching them remained strangely quiet. It wasn't easy but she resisted looking up to see his reaction.

"Okay, I give," Dylan said.

Angela jumped to her feet and backed away. Dylan went to stand and then came at her again. Angela had expected the move and swept her left leg out, kicking him in the chest and knocking him on his butt. He sprang to his feet and went for her again. Her concentration total, she was in full fighting mode. Nothing mattered other than surviving and putting the man in front of her on the floor. In her element, confidence sky-high, she was unbeatable. Nothing and no one could stop her now.

She never expected to be attacked from behind.

Jake wrapped his arms around Angela, holding back a groan as her slender, sexy body, covered only in spandex shorts, a sports bra, and a fine sheen of sweat, pressed against him. He'd never had her this close to him before and it was all he could do not to turn her around and taste those lips that had only moments ago been snarling at him. He'd always thought Angela was sexy as hell. Watching her take down a man who outweighed her by a hundred pounds was even sexier. He loved confident women. Angela was that and much more.

Stupid of him. While he was concentrating on what he wanted to do to her luscious body, she was poised to defend herself, determined to take him down. Jake was caught off guard when she stomped his foot and jammed her fist into his groin. The instant he let her go, she whirled around and gave him a good wallop on his jaw. He went down in an instant. She stood over him, her exotically beautiful face gazing down at him. Jake expected to see remorse or concern. He laughed out loud when he only saw triumph. She wasn't one bit regretful that she'd slammed him almost into unconsciousness. Damned if he didn't want to kiss her even more.

"I'd say you got your clock cleaned," Dylan said.

Getting to his feet, Jake nodded his approval. "I'd say you're right."

Angela glanced over at Dylan. "Did I pass the test or is there more?"

"You passed this one, but yeah, there's more."

Rubbing her hands against her hips as if preparing herself, she nodded. "Bring it on."

"How about giving Jake and me a few minutes to recover?"

She grinned at them both. "You think the killer's going to wait and let you recover?"

Both men laughed appropriately but Jake's amusement was greatly diminished by grim reality. In a couple of days, he and Angela could well be facing that killer. The police had no real knowledge of what this man looked like or if he was in any kind of fighting shape. Angela's skills might well put the man down with one blow but that didn't take away from the fact that she would be working to trap an evil, violent man whose priority was to abduct, torture, and then kill her. Jake had to keep her safe.

He turned to Dylan. "Why don't you take a breather and let me take this one?"

Dylan eyed him speculatively for a second and then nodded. "I'll go get some fresh air."

Jake turned to Angela and asked softly, "Think you've got it in you to take me down again?"

The door behind Angela closed with a resounding click. They were alone. Adrenaline flooded her veins like a gushing river. Fully aware that part of that surge had to do with the man she was about to spar with, she was determined to use that extra energy to her advantage.

Accepting his challenge with a slight smile, she waited to see what Jake would do. *Mistake.*

"You've got the most beautiful body." Blue eyes gleamed with fire as they slowly roamed up and down her body in a hot caress. "I've never seen anyone sexier."

Stunned into immobility, she barely noticed when he swooped. In an instant, she was slammed to the mat. Blocking her legs with his own, Jake pulled her wrists up, held them with one hand, and used his other hand to wrap around her neck.

Pinned and unable to move, Angela glared up at him. "That was a sneaky thing to do."

Instead of grinning down at her in triumph, he growled, "This isn't a game. The bastard is going to come at you with whatever he can to distract you. You've got to be ready for anything, at anytime. Understand?"

"Yes, of course I understand. It's just…"

"Just what?"

Her body betrayed her before she could control and hide her need. Sinking deeper into the mat, she shifted subtly, letting him settle more onto her. She saw the widening of his eyes just as he realized how their positions had changed. The physical response of his body was more revealing than his face, which remained impassive. The hard bulge pressing into her mound gave her the information she wanted.

He felt so good, more perfect than she ever imagined. Swallowing a moan of arousal, Angela closed her eyes as a wave of longing washed over her.

"Just what do you think you're doing?"

The harsh anger in his voice had her eyes open in a flash. "What do you mean?"

A grimace of pain passed across his face so quickly she might have missed it if she hadn't been watching him so closely. Without answering, he sprang to his feet.

If she hadn't been aching with need, she might have been impressed with the powerful athleticism of the move. Instead, Angela lay on the mat, breathless, aching, and once again feeling like a fool. How many times was she going to throw herself at this man before she got it through her head he wanted nothing like that between them? Just because he'd had an erection meant nothing. He was a man… men had erections all the time.

Feeling much older than she had only a few seconds ago, Angela rose to her feet. Jake was standing across the room, staring out the window. Stupid, but she felt as though she should apologize. She wouldn't. She had done nothing wrong. An invitation had been made and he had refused, once again.

She blew out a tired sigh. "I'm going to take a shower."

He whirled around and glared. "Like hell you will. We're still in the middle of a training session. Or have you forgotten that in a couple of days you're going to try to trap a killer?"

Outrage sent her spine poker straight. "I've forgotten nothing."

He came at her then, swift and lethal. A weapon, the same dummy knife Dylan had used, in his hand. The dark, fierce expression was back in place. She waited until he was half a foot away, timing it just so, then kicked out, knocking the knife from his hand. He reached for her but before he made contact, she stepped out of his way, whirled and then slammed her foot into his chest. Jake grunted, stumbled back, then came toward her once more. She blocked him again and then again. He wouldn't let up but neither would she.

The relentless look in his eyes told her he would keep going as long as she could. Angela was determined to prove him wrong. Minutes passed as they jabbed, kicked and swung at each other as if their lives depended upon it. Sweat poured from their overheated bodies, the entire atmosphere was tense and electric, alive with a frenetic, sizzling energy. The only sounds were the noises they made when their breath was knocked from them or gasps when one of them made a particularly good hit.

Breathless and trembling with exhaustion, she was teetering, struggling to stay on her feet when Dylan shouted behind her. "Dammit, that's enough!"

Jake dropped his hands. Angela had already committed to a punch, tried to pull back and failed. The blow to Jake's face was quick and fierce. She knew it had to have hurt but he barely flinched.

Breath sawed through her lungs so heavily, she could barely hear Dylan's furious voice. "What the hell did you think you were doing?"

Bent low, her hands on her knees, Angela raised her head and watched as Dylan railed at Jake.

They'd both gotten carried away. It wasn't all on Jake. In between gulps of breath, she said, "It was…my fault, too."

Dylan turned his glare on her and it took all of her willpower to not step back. This wasn't the low key LCR operative she was used to. He was furious with them both.

"I'll have a word with you in a few minutes. But let me say right now to both of you: You lose control like that again, I'll have Noah kick your asses off this case before you can blink. Your issues, whatever they are, have to go on the backburner." He paused a second, then said, "Got that?"

Jake silently blasted curses at himself. How had he allowed the situation to get so out of control? Angela was panting, close to dropping from exhaustion. That last blow she'd made to his face had been well deserved.

"It's my fault, not hers," he admitted gruffly.

"I don't care who's to blame. Don't let it happen again."

Jake gave a short, grim nod of acknowledgment. Being reamed out by Dylan was no big deal. He was a big boy, he could take the heat. However, Angela was taking some of the blame and he couldn't allow that to happen. This was all on him.

"I'm sorry, Angela." He hoped his eyes conveyed that his apology was for more than the too intense fighting session. She had offered her beautiful body and he had rejected her callously.

Her mouth trembled and then stretched into a grimace of a smile. "We were both wrong." Turning to Dylan, she said, "It won't happen again."

Dylan nodded. "Get cleaned up. We'll go to the shooting range this afternoon."

Jake watched as Angela grabbed a towel from the stack on the shelf and then left the room without another word.

The instant she was gone, Dylan turned to him. "What were you thinking?"

He hadn't been thinking, at least not with his brain. So turned on he could barely see straight, all of his sexual energy had been focused on fighting. He was damn glad Dylan interrupted them.

"I lost my head."

"You're sure you're going to be able to handle this?"

"Yes."

"I know how it feels to train someone you're attracted to. It can get damn uncomfortable. No one will think less of you for pulling out now. Once you're on the job, it'll be too late."

He shook his head. Nothing and no one would keep him from this mission.

Seeing the lingering doubt in the man's eyes, Jake said, "I might be a mixed-up son of a bitch but believe me, there's nothing more important to me than keeping Angela safe."

"I've been there," Dylan said. "Just make sure those feelings you're suppressing don't come out at the wrong time."

Suppressed feelings? Hell, if that were the only thing going on, he'd have no problem. But that was too mild a term for the volcano threatening to erupt inside him.

Jake grabbed a towel and swiped it down his face. "I'll see you on the shooting range this afternoon."

"Want to grab some lunch?"

Shaking his head, Jake backed away. "Thanks, but I've got some things to take care of."

He left the gym before Dylan could question him further. He needed a quiet place to detonate and then put himself back together. How had he let their training session get so out of hand? And Angela had been right there with him. If Dylan hadn't arrived when he did, who knows what might have happened?

He closed his eyes, swallowing a groan. He knew exactly what would have happened. They had been within seconds of ripping their clothes off and having each other on the floor. And he wanted that...more than anything he would have loved to lay her down, taste every inch of her taut, glistening skin and slide inside that beautiful body. But then what? Walk away and break her heart? Stay and break her heart? Either way, Angela got hurt. He'd been a jerk in a lot of areas of his life but risking Angela's heart went too far. Best thing he could do was get this job done to the best of his ability. He had told Dylan that protecting Angela was his number one priority. But that protection was not only from this freak that was killing women. It also included shielding her from assholes like himself.

*LCR Headquarters*

"He's driving me crazy."

Samara McCall sat across from Angela, amusement and affection gleaming in her eyes. "Men have a tendency to do that from time to time. I think it's part of their DNA."

Popping up from the chair she'd been sitting in, Angela paced around Samara's office. She couldn't seem to sit still. Maybe it was the anxiety and anticipation of working her first op. She had a feeling it had something to do with a certain hardheaded, too-sexy man.

They were supposed to be talking about whether she was mentally ready for her first op. Instead, all she had been able to focus on was Jake and that smoldering moment the day before.

"And it's not like I'm asking for a relationship with him or anything." The instant she saw Samara's eyebrows rise, she amended her statement. "Okay, yes. I want a relationship with him, but how does he know it wouldn't work out? He won't even give us a chance."

"Did he say why?"

Angela snorted softly. "Of course not. That would involve actually talking about himself."

"So I guess he doesn't know that you're aware of his background."

She dropped back into her chair with a sigh. "I've known the background of almost every operative since Noah hired me. Never once have I felt guilty about it."

"But you feel guilty now?"

"Yes." She glanced over at her non-judgmental friend. "I should have told him from the beginning. Shouldn't I?"

"What do you think?"

She jumped back up and resumed her pacing. "Of course I should have told him. But how do you tell a man who's intent on never telling you his past that you already know all of his secrets?"

A furrow appeared on Samara's forehead. "You didn't delve into his past because you were nosey. You did it because it's your job. That's definitely not the same thing."

"I know, it's just that it's obvious he doesn't want me to know."

"Then yes, at some point, you should tell him so you can get it behind you."

"But not yet?"

"If you think that would inhibit this mission, then no. If not..." Samara shrugged.

"Do you think Noah put us together to...you know, put us together?"

Samara gave a startled laugh. "I have no idea. He rarely discusses those kinds of things with me. I asked him once if he pairs his operatives with that purpose in mind."

"What did he say?"

"Just that when he sees two people who have a chemistry together, it makes for a good team. What they choose to do with that chemistry once the op is over is up to them."

She had a feeling she knew what Jake would want to do with their chemistry, especially since he refused to even acknowledge they had any. He would ruthlessly suppress it until it smothered.

"So, now that we've talked about Jake and his hard-headedness, talk to me about how you're doing in other areas. Sleeping better?"

"Much better." After her family's death, she had slept in fits and spurts. Now, though not always sleeping the entire night, she was finally getting some solid shuteye.

"What did you decide to do with your parents' house?"

That had been hanging over her head for the past six months. Her parents had moved there when she was ten, when her family had first moved to Paris. She loved the house, but it was the people who had lived there that she adored. They might be gone but the wonderful memories remained. She had been unable to make a decision on selling it. "I'm still debating."

"It's hard to let go," Samara said softly.

She doubted if she could ever truly let go. A few days ago, she'd ventured into her sister's bedroom. In seconds, she was lying on Chloe's bed and sobbing into her pillow like a baby. The scent of her sister's shampoo had been there but was fading. How she had loved Chloe's infectious laugh and optimistic attitude. And Max, who had always been awkward and shy around everyone but his family, had been coming out of his shell.

"You okay?"

Angela jerked her head up and blinked back tears. Convincing Samara she was mentally sound enough to endure the rigors of a mission by breaking down was probably a very bad move. It didn't matter that she and Noah's wife had been the closest of friends for over three years. If she didn't think Angela could handle the op, she'd have no problem advising Noah to pull her off the case.

"I'm fine. Really I am."

"Tell me what you were just thinking."

"Chloe and Max. They barely had a chance to live."

"They adored their big sister."

Her smile feeling somewhat fractured, she nodded. "The feeling was mutual. I went to the house the other day. Broke down in Chloe's room."

"Tears can wash away a ton of grief."

"If that's the case, I should be sparkling clean."

"Bottom line. Can you do this job? No one would think less of you if you chose to wait."

Doubts were part of being human and Angela wasn't immune to them. However, when it came to her belief in her abilities, she had no doubts. She had been training for this job all her adult life.

"Without a doubt, I can do the job."

Samara regarded her for several seconds. Angela withstood the look, knowing her friend would make the assessment regardless of their relationship. Finally, she nodded and said, "I'll tell Noah you're ready."

"I thought it would be tougher to convince you."

"I've watched you deal with a grief that would debilitate many people. Our talk today was more formality than an evaluation."

Angela breathed out a relieved sigh. Samara had been her last hurdle and though she hadn't worried she could convince her she was ready, to know that her friend had that kind of faith in her increased her confidence even more. Now she would go home and prepare. Jake had said if things went well with Samara, they would leave tomorrow afternoon for London.

"So I'll see you when I get back."

For the first time, Samara's worry showed. Holding out her arms for a hug, she said, "Don't take any chances. Okay?"

Reaching down to her petite friend, she returned the embrace. "Don't worry. Your husband trained me well."

"I hope you can be home for Micah's birthday party. He would be so disappointed if he didn't get to see his favorite aunt on his special day."

"That's four weeks away. I'll be back before then I'm sure."

She could feel Samara's eyes on her as she walked out the door. A shiver of apprehension zipped up her spine. For the first time, a ripple of doubt entered her head. Was she being stupid? Should she tell Noah she would sit this one out and take another, less dangerous mission? She instantly knew the answer. She could do this job.

Now having Jake Mallory as a partner? That was a completely different matter.

# Chapter Six

*Two days later*

*London, England*

"You're going to wear a hole in the carpet if you don't stop pacing."

"I don't see why we can't go out. He hasn't seen me yet."

"No, and he doesn't need to see you."

"I thought that was the whole plan."

"It is the plan, when the time is right."

When she blew out an explosive sigh, Jake said patiently, "Look, we know he likes a type, with a certain occupation. If he's roaming around and sees you today, he might not take the bait if he sees you again at the club. The man might be certifiably insane but he's not stupid. He's got to know the police are going to use undercover people to try to trap him. If he suspects anything at all, we'll have to start all over again."

He was right, but she was going stir-crazy. Jake had been sitting in that chair for over two hours, reading. She'd always thought a man who read was incredibly sexy, so watching a man she already thought was sexy read a book didn't help. And when he'd put his reading glasses on? She'd almost drooled.

She had brought her own books but hadn't cracked one open. Concentrating in such close proximity to Jake was impossible. She told herself she could leave the room, even leave the apartment. They had rented the apartment attached to this one, too. That way if the killer began stalking her, he would believe she lived alone. There was a door inside the apartment that led to the other one. She could go there and get away from him. So why the hell didn't she?

Ignoring the silent, damning question, she asked aloud, "What time is our meeting with the club owner?"

Without looking up from the page, he answered, "Six o'clock."

She headed to the miniscule kitchen. "Want something to eat?"

Hearing a heavy sigh, she turned to see that he'd finally put his book down and taken his glasses off. That didn't help because now that single-minded focus was concentrated solely on her.

"What's the real problem?"

"I'm just anxious to get started."

"Are you nervous about your undercover role? If you are, we can change it. Since we're meeting with the club owner, all you have to do is tell him you want to do something else. You could be a waitress like Riley. You don't have to dance."

Riley and Justin would be working in the club, too. Riley would be waiting tables and Justin was the new bouncer. Having them as additional protection gave her a deeper feeling of security. And though Riley was more petite than his preferred victim, Angela knew the operative would play a role in hopes of attracting the killer.

"Angela?" Jake broke into her musings. "Want to change your cover?"

She shook her head. Was she nervous about taking her clothes off in front of dozens of drunken men? Of course she was. She wasn't shy about her body but neither was she used to flaunting it nakedly to strangers either. That three of those people weren't strangers but co-workers added another layer of concern. However, this was her job. LCR missions often involved roles that would make the average person uncomfortable. Angela was determined that she could be just as professional as any other operative.

"I'll be fine…as long as no one gets too close."

A fierce, hot look flashed in his eyes. "No one will lay a hand on you, I promise you that."

"Yes, well… They'll be sliding money into my unmentionables, so there will be hands touching me. Besides, you can't be too protective or he'll never take the bait."

"You let me worry about that."

"Did you ever have to deal with a serial killer when you were a cop?"

His "Back off" expression firmly in place, he shook his head.

That was a look she'd seen many times and had gotten used to. It didn't matter. She was made of sterner stuff. She'd just keep asking questions until he finally opened up.

"You were a cop for what…six years? I'm sure you dealt with some terrible people during that time."

His face grew harder and Angela shivered. Okay, maybe she wasn't immune to those blue eyes piercing through her. They had known each other for months now and the only events he had talked to her about were the things that had happened to him since he had come to Paris. It was as if he wanted to pretend he had never had a life before LCR. Problem was, that life he wanted to pretend never existed continued to eat at him.

"You can give me those looks all day long but it doesn't mean I'll stop asking questions."

"Why? What is it that you feel you have to know about me?"

Should she take this was as an opportunity to tell him she knew almost everything about him? He had to know that she knew a little. Why else would she ask him about being a cop? That was information he certainly hadn't shared with her. But should she tell him she knew about his wife's death? That he blamed himself was apparent, but she knew the whole story. Teresa Mallory's death had been a horrific tragedy and many were at fault. Jake was not one of them.

No, an inevitable argument would ensue. They didn't need the distraction. After this was over, she would come clean. She should have long ago but had never got to the point of saying, "I know everything about you and I think you're a wonderful man."

She shrugged. "You said we were friends. Friends know about each other's lives."

"There's still a lot I don't know about you."

She almost laughed. After all the chattering she'd done, there was almost nothing he didn't already know. Still, if there were questions he wanted to ask, she was ready, willing, and able to give him answers.

"What do you want to know?"

"Were you born in Paris?"

"No. My father was French, my mother is...was from America...she grew up in Wisconsin. She met my father while she was on holiday in Europe. He moved to the States when they were married. I was born in Milwaukee but we moved to Paris when I was ten."

"So that's why you have so many Americanisms."

She smiled. "We rarely spoke French in our house. My mother never learned to speak the language and my father was fluent in English. We were a very American family living in the heart of Paris."

"Your brother and sister were born in France?"

"No, but they were just infants when we moved to Paris. However, they learned to speak both languages equally well."

"Did your parents know that you worked for LCR?"

She shook her head. "I hated keeping the truth from them but Noah feared for their safety. And I didn't want to worry them. He and I agreed that I would be as vague as possible about my employment. I think they were under the impression that I worked for an aging hippy."

"Because of your tattoos and piercings?"

"Yes."

"They didn't know they were fake?"

She swallowed a startled breath. "How could you tell? People who have known me for years don't know that. Even Noah didn't know for a long time."

"Maybe that's because he—"

"Because he what?"

Looking as though he wanted to bite his tongue off, Jake shrugged and looked away as he murmured, "Maybe it's because he hasn't looked at you as closely as I have."

A flash of heat rushed through her. Though she would love to take this conversation to a different level, she wouldn't. Jake had made it clear he wanted nothing between them and while she refused to accept the finality of that, she wouldn't pursue it here. When this case was over though, she planned to pursue the hell out of it.

"When I was hired, I was sporting a couple of fake tats. Just experimenting to see how I liked them. Noah told me my number one priority would be to deter uninvited visitors to LCR. So, when it came time to report for my first day on the job, I showed up with so many piercings and tats, Noah barely recognized me."

"Did he ask you why you'd added them?"

"No, funnily enough, he didn't. Noah has always been accepting of my differences."

"You're very fond of him, aren't you?"

"Absolutely. Without him and Milo hiring me, I'm not sure how my family and I would have survived."

"Milo's the guy who helped McCall put LCR together?"

"Yes, he was killed by an LCR traitor."

"Hard to believe there are those who betray Last Chance Rescue, knowing what we do."

"Unfortunately there are people who would sell their own souls for money."

Jake released a dry, humorless laugh. "Yeah, don't I know that."

"You've run across a lot of people like that?"

"Hell yeah, haven't you?"

"Actually no. Most of the people I know are good, decent people. Learning we had a traitor in our midst was a shock."

"You're lucky. Most of the people I've known were out for one thing only—themselves. And to hell with everyone else."

"That's a very jaded view of life. Do you include LCR people in your assessment?"

"No. I know none of them are angels but from what I've observed they're not in this line of work for the power and money most people desire. They genuinely want to help others."

"Just like you."

He got to his feet and headed to the kitchen. "Want something to drink?"

An exasperated sigh, laced with sadness, escaped her. Typical Jake move. If the conversation got the least bit personal, he shut it down or walked away.

She had stopped wondering what made her pursue a man who made it obvious he didn't want the attention. It wasn't sheer stubbornness, although she had that in abundance, nor was it wanting what she couldn't have. She had been attracted to other men, some had returned her interest, others hadn't. None had fascinated her like Jake. Not one of them had made her want to hold and comfort him. Nor had any of them infuriated and turned her on at the same time. Her heart had no doubts that Jake was the one for her. She did, however, have serious doubts that her heart would get what it wanted.

"I have another question."

She looked up as Jake returned to the room, a glass of water in his hand. "What?"

"Why a stripper?"

She was more than a little surprised he hadn't asked the question before. The disapproval on his face when he'd looked at her cover had been apparent.

"Exotic dancers are one of his preferences. It only made sense that one of us go undercover as one."

"I agree. But why you? You set up the covers for most LCR operatives. You could have assigned dancer to someone else."

"The other female operatives on the mission don't have the experience I have."

It took every ounce of control she possessed not to laugh at his stunned expression.

"You've been a stripper?"

"Not technically but I took some classes."

"When?"

"Exotic dance class was an elective in college and I really enjoyed it. After I graduated, I took more classes to stay in shape. It's a great workout. My body is as limber now as it was when I was in school."

Jake clenched his jaw. Hell, that was information he definitely didn't want. He'd been throwing out questions at her, hoping for relief from the ache that was a constant part of him when he was with Angela. Her revelations about her exotic dance experience were ones he could have done without. Just the thought of her beautiful, graceful body, barely clothed and dancing sensually to music, made him rock hard. What the hell was he going to do when he actually witnessed the event?

He took a long swallow of his cold water. The temperature outside was just above freezing. In this room, it had shot up considerably in the last few seconds.

"I'm going to shower." She stood and smiled slightly. "All of my tats are just about gone. None of the victims were inked, so I figured I needed to get rid of them."

"So none of them were real?"

"And no piercings either." She easily pulled an earring from her earlobe that he could have sworn was pierced. Laughter dancing in her eyes, she added, "I have an aversion to needles."

"That's something we have in common. I can't stand them either." He grinned as he remembered one drunken night long ago. "I was on leave with a few of my buddies from the Army. One night we were hell bent on getting tattoos. I thought I was just drunk enough that I could go through with it. Got in the chair and they brought the needle out. Didn't take long for me to realize that no matter how much alcohol I consumed, I would never be drunk enough to voluntarily get stuck with a needle. Everybody but me got a tat that night." He shook his head. "I liked to have never lived that down."

That was probably more than he'd ever told her about his past. He tensed, waiting for the inevitable questions. They were there…he saw them sparkling in her eyes. But, as usual, Angela did what she always did—the unexpected. Instead of pursuing the subject, she shrugged. "It's probably best that I don't have any. Tattoos and piercings might have been a distraction."

Considering that everyone would probably have their tongues hanging out watching that gorgeous body strip bare, Jake figured few would have noticed body art or piercings. Angela's body was a work of art all by itself.

She stretched, revealing a slender, toned torso and then worked her neck back and forth. "I'm a little tense. Hopefully the shower will loosen me up. If I get to dance tonight, I need to be as limber as possible."

Jake's eyes followed her hungrily as she walked out of the room. An email ping from his laptop was a welcomed distraction. Twisting the laptop around, he clicked the email icon and sighed when he saw the sender. Even after all these years, his mother had yet to let go of the idea that the life she wanted for her son wasn't the life he wanted for himself.

Weekly, if not daily, she sent newsy emails, detailing what was going on in their pocket of the world. Jake had learned to break down the information, picking out the parts that updated him on his family without paying attention to all the society news his mother liked to impart. He enjoyed the updates on his parents but could care less about the other stuff.

He had played that game once—gone to the right schools, associated with the kids that met his parents' approval, dated the most suitable girls. And he'd almost married one of those girls. The only rebellion he'd ever had was his choice in careers. His parents had wanted him to join the family business. Instead he'd gone into the Army and then the police force. The latter had been a bad decision since it'd had so many negative consequences. His job as a cop had gotten Teresa killed, cost another woman her life, and had virtually destroyed his own life. Yeah, a damn bad decision.

"Did you read the email from Noah?"

He glanced over his shoulder and felt a gut punch all the way to his groin. Angela stood at the entrance to the living room dressed in nothing but a towel. He knew he'd be seeing her in a lot less very soon but had planned to be prepared by then.

Tearing his eyes away from the vision, he turned back to his computer and clicked a few keys to go to another email account. She came to stand beside him, so close he could feel her breath on his neck. His eyes narrowed, focusing on the screen in front of him. Dammit, did she not know what she was doing to him?

Another ping came from the laptop, indicating that he did indeed have a new email from McCall. Clicking on, he cursed softly as he read the terse message: *Missing woman found this morning. Same cause of death. You have a five-to-ten day window to get this bastard's attention before he grabs another victim. Let's make sure he takes our bait.*

"It's just so sad. A family is learning the awful fate of a loved one. And if we're not successful in trapping him, another woman will soon be going through the same horror. We have to stop him, Jake."

Bracing himself for the effect she always had on him, he turned to face her. He had been prepared for her beauty, not the tears swimming in her eyes. Telling himself he was only going to offer comfort, he reached for her. Suddenly she was in his arms, in his lap, and he was holding her.

Slender arms wrapped around his shoulders, a soft as silk face lay against his neck. She felt so damned good. Better than any fantasy he'd ever allowed himself. He swallowed hard and kept his arms loose around her. This was about offering his support and friendship. It had nothing to do with his inappropriate lust.

"Jake?" Warm breath from her soft whisper was like an erotic caress against his skin.

His entire body went taut as a violin string. Eyes closed, teeth clenched, Jake fought every instinct and signal his body was sending him. He told himself she needed comfort. He told himself he had nothing to give her. He told himself to let her go.

Her lips pressed against his throat in a hot open-mouthed erotic invitation.

Ignoring every warning in his head, Jake went for what he wanted above all else. Lowering his head, he trailed tender kisses along her impossibly soft cheek. When she turned to look up at him, her dark eyes holding a hunger he felt deep within his soul, he could no more have let her go than he could stop breathing. Groaning with pent-up desire, his mouth covered hers.

His world exploded.

Never had he tasted anything as delicately delicious or more decadent. She had the softest, sweetest mouth in the universe and Jake wanted to devour every succulent morsel. Her mouth opened beneath his with a blatant challenge to explore. Accepting the provocation, he thrust deep and lost his mind.

While he ravaged her mouth, Jake's hands were equally busy exploring. The towel trapped between their bodies was an irritating deterrent to his goals. Growling his frustration, he lifted his head to concentrate his energies and finally tugged it low enough to expose her breasts. Hungrily, his gaze roamed over her, devouring the perfect globes of cream satin with small, rose-colored nipples.

Taking a breast in his hand, he tested the weight against his palm, then flicked her nipple with his thumb and watched in awe as it went tauter, stiffer, seeming to beg for his mouth. Unable to resist, he swirled his tongue around the tight peak. Pulling away slightly, he admired the now glistening and even tighter bud. "Damn, that's pretty."

A soft, gasping sigh had him moving his gaze from the most perfect breast he'd ever seen to the most beautiful face in existence. Classically high cheekbones, velvet brown eyes, full wide lips and slightly pointed chin, was the type of beauty poets wrote sonnets about. Jake had no poetry in him. The only thing he possessed in spades was pure, unadulterated lust.

Leaving the vision of her face for a moment, his gaze explored her body. Long... impossibly long, sleek legs, ivory-colored and toned, led down to narrow feet with nails painted a vibrant red.

Breathing out a longing sigh, he growled hoarsely, "You are so damned beautiful."

Shuddering with arousal, Angela watched Jake's face as she lay in his arms. Wanting to take the initiative, wanting to give everything and anything he asked for, she waited for a sign of acceptance. This man had rejected her more than once. Having him do so while she was almost nude and vulnerable in his arms wasn't something she could survive. If she tried to take it further than what he was ready to give, the fracture in her heart would widen to a giant crevice.

So, she waited. Hoping against hope that this time he would want what she wanted. That at last the barrier would be broken and he would allow his need to take control. Her eyes met his and she knew the answer before he said the words, "I could hurt you so easily, Angela. I don't want to be the one to break your heart."

She tried to smile though she knew it was a poor attempt. "Ever thought you should be worried about your own heart and not mine?"

"What would hurt me more than anything would be to hurt you."

"Why don't you let me worry about that?"

"I'm not a forever kind of guy. Not anymore."

"Who said anything about forever? What's wrong with living in the moment… the here and now?"

"You're not a living in the moment kind of woman."

"And you think you know what kind of woman I am?"

Before he could answer, Angela was sitting up and struggling to get away from him. She needed distance or she was going to say or do something that she would eventually regret. Neither punching him in the nose for his arrogance nor kissing him because she saw the hurt and sadness behind his words were the right courses to take.

Only Jake wasn't having it. His arms tightened around her, keeping her from leaving.

"Let me go, Jake."

"I can't."

"Why? If you don't want me, then let me go."

"Hell woman, you think I don't want you?" He shook her gently, his eyes blazing into hers. The evidence of his desire was hard against her hip. "I've never wanted anyone the way I want you. That's what makes this so damned dangerous."

Her heart zinged with joy but the anger in his eyes quickly squelched the happiness. "Dangerous? How?"

Apparently regretting his words, he shook his head and loosened his hold on her. "Forget it. It doesn't matter."

"It matters to me."

Pushing her gently out of his arms, he glanced at the clock. "You'd better get dressed. We're due at the club in an hour."

She stood in front of him. The towel bunched at her waist, her breasts still exposed. She wanted to shout at him for being so damned stubborn. She wanted to cry because once again she had allowed him to reject her.

His eyes looking everywhere but at her, Jake growled, "Dammit, go get some clothes on."

She wasn't embarrassed by her nudity. Soon, Jake would be seeing her dressed in almost nothing and gyrating on a stage as if she were in the throes of sexual ecstasy. Still, she felt vulnerable and open, exposed in a way she wouldn't be in her stripper garb.

Before she turned away, she needed him to understand one thing. "This is the last time, Jake. I've made more advances to you than I've done with all the other men I've known, combined. You've turned me down for the last time. I'm through offering."

Turning, she walked away. With every step she took, she wanted him to call her back. When she reached the door and there was no sound coming from him, she released the breath she had been holding. That was it. She had spoken the truth, she wouldn't offer again.

# Chapter Seven

*Club Drago*

*London*

Jake opened the door for Angela and then followed her into the club. After she'd walked away from him an hour ago, he'd been cursing his poor handling of the situation, sure that things would now be awkward, possibly putting the mission in jeopardy. But Angela was a true professional, making him admire her all the more. The moment she'd walked out of the bedroom, dressed for their meeting with the club manager, she'd acted as if nothing had happened.

For someone who was doing his best to protect a woman he cared for so deeply, he was doing a shitty job of it. He'd damned well better get his head out of his ass when it came time to protecting her physically. Hadn't he already learned his lesson the hard way?

"Think I'll be able to dance tonight?" Angela asked.

"Depends. Roddy, the manager, is totally onboard with our mission but if he puts you on in place of someone who's scheduled, it might look suspicious."

She held up her purse. "I brought my outfit and music, just in case."

"In that?" The handbag barely looked big enough to carry her wallet and apartment keys.

She glanced down at her legs. "I'm wearing my boots. The rest of my costume is minimal. Remember, I'm a stripper. The clothing tends to be quite small."

Yeah, like he was going to forget. Jake's jaw tightened. He'd almost not survived having an almost nude Angela in his arms. Now he was going to sit in an audience while strangers ogled her. This would be the most hellish LCR assignment he'd ever been on.

"May I help you?" A young woman dressed in a sedate brown pantsuit came toward them.

"We're here to see Roddy. The name's Jake, this is Angela."

"Of course, he told me to send you to his office when you arrived."

As they followed the woman through the club to the office, Jake saw Angela stare at the stage and the tall silver pole in the center of it. Was she nervous? Though she seemed to have the energy of three normal people, Jake didn't see Angela as a nervous person. But still, anyone would be apprehensive to have to dance almost nude in front of strangers, wouldn't they?

"You okay?" he asked.

"Yes, just trying to decide the best routine for the stage size. It's not very large so most of my moves will have to be done with the pole." She nodded as if satisfied with her assessment and then turned to him. He was stunned to see excitement gleaming in her eyes. "I'm really good on the pole."

*Holy hell, he was in trouble.*

Roddy Rawlins was a short, stubby man with a raspy voice, tobacco-stained teeth and wise eyes. Without any seeming sexuality in his gaze, he assessed Angela as an employee and nodded approvingly.

"I understand you have pole dancing experience?"

"Yes." Experience might be stretching it a bit since she'd never danced in a club. This would be very different from the gym where she had taken her classes. However, she had two things in her favor—skill and confidence. Her instructor, a former exotic dancer, had told her she was a natural. And though Angela knew she was far from perfect, she had the confidence to see this through. Would some of it make her uncomfortable? Absolutely. But in this case, the end definitely justified the means.

"Mr. McCall assured me you would fit in well. Normally I wouldn't have room for another dancer, but one of my ladies quit two days ago. You can take her spot."

"I brought my costume and music. I'm prepared to go on tonight."

"Excellent." He beamed approval and then, all business, leaned forward and said, "House rules are simple but strictly enforced. Customers aren't allowed to touch, other than a hand slipping money into your garter or panties. Tops come off, bottoms are optional. Your call."

Though she wasn't looking at him, she felt Jake's body tense up. Would he see her differently once she began to dance? And if so, would that be a good difference or bad? She gave a mental shrug. There was no point in worrying about that now. Besides, catching this lunatic trumped damaging their non-existent romance.

"How comfortable are you with lap dances?" Roddy asked.

The thought of sitting on some stranger's lap and rubbing up against him sent shudders through her. There was only one man she wanted to do that with. "It's something I'd prefer not to do. Is that all right?"

"Sure, but be prepared to get requests because most of the ladies offer this service. It's a good money maker."

"Maybe it'll make her seem more mysterious and less approachable," Jake said. "Something like that could piss off the killer."

Roddy nodded slowly. "That's a possibility. Half of my customers are regulars who come in two or three nights a week. The other half includes men on business trips, bachelor parties, and the occasional passerby who want entertainment with their alcohol. But we state clearly on our marquis that lap dances are available for an extra charge."

"Is pissing him off the right way to go?" Angela asked.

Jake shrugged. "Could be. If he gets so anxious he can't control himself, he might make a mistake. It's worth a try."

"Then it's a go. No lap dances for…" Roddy turned back to Angela. "What's your stage name?"

Silly, but this had been the most difficult thing to decide. A name could have a visceral impact on the killer, forming the image of what he wanted her to be in his mind. Would calling herself one thing instead of another make him see her as his next victim or scare him away to go after someone else? In the end, she'd decided she was over-thinking and had come up with something easy that worked for her.

"Dark Angel," she said.

"Excellent. We don't have anything similar right now. Our ladies get along well. There's the occasional blow-up, but most of the time, they're focused on giving the best performances possible."

"How many times will I dance each night?"

"Twice if everyone shows up. Three times max." Roddy turned to Jake again. "And your role is new owner. Right?"

Jake nodded. Martin Tabor, the owner of Club Drago was an acquaintance of Noah's. Tabor had agreed to make it appear he'd sold the club to an American businessman. Jake's presence would simply look like a new owner enjoying his newest business acquisition.

"I'll stay in the audience, walk around a bit. It'll give me a chance to assess everyone without seeming suspicious." He tilted his head toward Angela. "My top priority is making sure she stays safe."

Roddy nodded. "That'll work fine but I've got one question, mate."

"What's that?" Jake asked.

"Are you going to be able to handle it when men make sexual comments about your woman?"

Why would Roddy assume she was Jake's woman? She was about to explain that this wasn't the case when Jake muttered, "I'll handle it."

Angela swallowed a gasp. No denial that she wasn't his woman. And the grimness of his tone gave her shivers. Whatever Jake's reasons for not wanting to take their relationship to a sexual level, he definitely had strong feelings about having other men seeing her nude.

Roddy nodded. "I'll hold you to that. I want this killer caught too but having you disrupt business is out of the question."

Business was business, both she and Jake understood that concept.

She stood and held out her hand. "Thank you, Mr. Rawlins. We'll do our best to have no impact on your business."

For the first time Roddy gave her a look of pure lust, his eyes oozing up and down her body like thick slime. "Oh, I think you'll have an impact on the business but it will all be very good." If possible, the tone of his voice was even slimier than his look.

Wanting to put their discussion back on a business-like basis, she chose to take his words as a compliment. Maintaining a pleasant and neutral expression, she kept her hand outstretched.

The sleazy expression disappeared and Roddy smiled congenially as he gave a firm, business-like handshake. "You're going to do just fine."

It had been a test. Angela was glad she had passed it.

"What time do I go on and where's the dressing room?"

"You're on at nine and then at ten-thirty. Be back here by seven-thirty. That'll give you some time to get a look around and the chance to meet the other ladies before your first performance."

She felt Jake at her back as they left Roddy's office, went through the club and out into the early evening. Traffic was at a fever pitch with car horns blaring and the occasional zoom of a vehicle that managed to get out of the gridlock.

"You want to get some dinner or go back to the apartment?" Jake asked.

Go back to the apartment so soon after what had happened earlier? No freaking way. "Let's eat, I'm starving."

The relief on his face obvious, he said, "There's a good Italian restaurant a couple of blocks up."

Angela silently followed him down the street. She shouldn't be hurt that he didn't want to go back to the apartment. This job was not about her unrequited love, it was about saving lives. The sting of his rejection would fade. This was her first LCR op and she was determined to do the best job she could. Jake was her partner and handler. To expect something more from him was not only unprofessional, it was silly. She was out to catch a killer, not get laid.

With that cemented in her mind, she managed to carry on a halfway intelligent conversation about the various Italian recipes she'd learned in a cooking class. So intent on acting as if nothing was bothering her, she hardly noticed that the discussion was all one-sided.

*How are you going to handle men making sexual comments about your woman?* The question reverberated through Jake's head. The fact that Roddy had read him correctly should bother him but he had bigger concerns. The brief taste the man had given of just one slime-ball stare made him realize he wasn't as detached as he had told himself he would be. Jake was a born protector—a trait that had occasionally driven Teresa crazy. He knew the vile things people could do to each other and had wanted to keep her safe. In the end, he had failed miserably.

Protecting Angela was going to be doubly difficult. Not only would he have to restrain himself from going after the men in the club, he also had to be on the lookout for the crazed madman who might want to kill her. And his feelings for her, whether he wanted to admit them or not, weren't the mildly affectionate ones he told himself he could allow. The things she made him feel were gut deep and full of all the emotions he'd denied himself for years.

But they had to be shoved back, out of the way. These kinds of feelings weren't something he could allow, especially on an op.

They walked into the small mom and pop Italian restaurant he'd eaten at a couple of times when he'd been vacationing here. Angela had chattered nonstop since they'd left the club, seemingly unaware of his lack of words.

They were seated and had placed their order before Jake spoke. Wanting to get the discussion back to an easygoing non-confrontational status they'd developed over the last few months, Jake said, "I ate here a couple of times when I was on vacation. I think you'll like it."

Stupid to forget that Angela was the queen of confrontations.

Leaning forward, she seared him with her eyes and said softly, "So, *am* I your woman, Jake?"

# CHAPTER EIGHT

*A house outside London*

"You really shouldn't be afraid of me. I'm going to make you famous. When I'm through with you, everyone in England will know who you are."

The silver tape across Clarissa Eaton's mouth muffled her responding sob. Her eyes spoke for her. They looked upon him as if he were the devil himself. Her fear exuded a healthy respect. He liked that. She also had the appearance of a terrified lamb. That was proper and very important. Suffering for one's art was part of the process. Of course, she didn't understand that yet. Once she did, they would get along famously.

"You should feel honored that you were chosen. I don't normally invite women like you into my world. I'm very particular about my preferences. And you aren't even from my usual hunting area. You caught my attention one day and I haven't been able to think of anyone since."

Dark green eyes, drenched with tears, blinked up at him. Once again they spoke volumes, telling him she wasn't honored. That would change though. Before their final goodbye, she would learn many important lessons. All of his women had left him with the knowledge of his greatness in their eyes. So would this one.

Her eye color was a disappointment. From a distance, they had looked brown. Once he began the process of elevation to her new status, they would have to be covered. They could prove a distraction; one he couldn't afford. Every nuance of the process was carefully calculated. If even one aspect was off, it would ruin everything.

A common man would either discard her or remove the distraction. He was not a common man. He had chosen her for a reason. Just because he didn't know why yet didn't mean she was a mistake. Knowledge would come. And so he would proceed. When it was time, the answer would be revealed to him.

Taking the scissors from the drawer, he held them up to the light, loving the way they glinted like diamonds. He looked down at Clarissa again. At the sight of his scissors, her green eyes blazed with terror. Hmm. Perhaps the color wasn't so bad after all.

With that comforting thought, he began to cut, Clarissa's muffled screams sounding like thunderous applause as they hit his ears.

*Club Drago*

"You nervous?" a gravelly female voice asked.

As soon as Angela entered the dressing room, Georgette Hilliard, stage name Dynamite, had taken her under her wing. Georgette was the oldest dancer at Club Drago and apparently saw herself as a surrogate big sister.

Georgette's question surprised her because it made her realize that she *was* nervous. Nerves weren't usually an issue for her but this was so completely out of the norm for her low-key lifestyle, she couldn't stop the army of butterflies battling each other in her stomach.

Reading the correct answer in Angela's expression, Georgette said, "Don't worry, Sweets. Once you're on stage, the nerves will disappear. It's dark out in the club. When the lights come on, you just go to your happy place and let the music take over."

Good advice except she wasn't performing for the reason most exotic dancers went on stage. She was performing to catch a killer. That was definitely something they hadn't covered in her dance classes.

Apparently seeing the doubt in her eyes, Georgette offered another avenue. "You have a man?"

Did she? Her question to Jake had been met with a bright blue gaze of pure heat that had almost incinerated her insides. She shouldn't have asked the question in the first place. Sometimes her tongue overpowered her brain and she blurted out inappropriate questions. Asking hadn't worked anyway—Jake hadn't answered. Passionate intensity had been in his expression but the words she longed to hear never came.

Still, whether he looked upon her as his woman, Angela knew one thing—Jake was her man, whether he wanted to admit to it or not.

"Yes, I have a man."

"Think about him. Pretend it's just you and him and you're dancing only for him. With your body and exotic looks, you'll have men salivating. Add that kind of personal touch, make each man believe you're dancing only for him." She nodded knowingly. "They'll be throwing money at your feet."

The money would go to charity, so that was a good thing. And thinking about Jake while she danced? That was excellent advice. What better way for her to show him how much she wanted him, especially since she doubted she would ever get the chance to dance for him in private.

"Thank you, Georgette. I appreciate the advice."

"New girl?"

Angela turned around and faced a petite, large-breasted woman with bleached hair teased up so high it easily gave her three more inches of height. Her costume consisted of an extremely short cowgirl dress and cowboy boots.

Georgette nodded. "Angela, this is Luscious Lucy. She goes on right before you do."

Lucy flashed a bright, welcoming smile. "I'll warm them up for you."

"Thanks," Angela said, returning her smile.

A voice boomed behind them. "Lucy, you're on in two."

Lucy gave a teasing wink. "Better head that way before Arlo has a nervous breakdown."

Angela had met Arlo, the stage manager, earlier. He was a thin, nervous man with a beaky nose and kind eyes. Georgette had introduced them and then explained that Arlo was married to a former dancer of Club Drago. She said he had a fatherly affection for all the girls and watched out for them.

As Lucy swayed toward the door in her four-inch cowboy boots, Angela stood and surveyed herself in the full-length mirror.

"There are going to be some hot and bothered men out there tonight," Georgette said admiringly.

Perhaps, but there were only two she wanted to attract. One was the love of her life and the other was a sadistic killer.

Jake sat at a table, on a dais to the left of the stage, with an excellent view of the club. So far, he'd seen nothing out of the ordinary. Just everyday, average horny men staring with lust-glazed eyes as beautiful and scantily clad women gyrated in front of them.

The audience was mostly men of varying ages. He saw a few guys who didn't look old enough to be there, along with a couple of old geezers who looked as though they could keel over at anytime. None of them looked like killers, serial or otherwise. But then, mild-mannered looking people committed bloodcurdling crimes every damn day.

Ingram and Kelly had started their undercover jobs tonight, too. Dressed in a short, red skirt, a white, midriff-baring top and stilettos that made her appear about five inches taller, the always serious-looking Riley Ingram was barely recognizable. Jake had never worked with the young operative before and had to admit he was impressed with her acting abilities. The few times he'd met her, she'd seemed withdrawn and closed off. Tonight she was the total opposite. She flirted and laughed, deterring wayward hands and off-color comments with impressive diplomacy.

Justin Kelly stood at attention a few yards from her. Though his eyes roamed the crowded room, the former special ops man returned his gaze frequently to his partner. Other than her height, Riley had many of the same similarities as the killer's preferred victim. Even though the two operatives were mainly here for Angela's protection, Riley Ingram would also be working hard to attract the killer's attention. And Justin Kelly would be doing the same thing as Jake—looking for a killer and making sure his partner stayed safe.

Jake had worked an op with Kelly a couple of months ago. Their mission had been to rescue a small group of aid workers being held for ransom in Guatemala. He'd been impressed with Kelly's no-bullshit attitude. They'd gone in just before dawn and grabbed the five victims. No casualties and the disorganized group of small-time thugs were now locked up. It had been a good day.

As the countrified and well-endowed Lucy left the stage wearing only her G-string and cowboy boots, the music started for the next performer. Jake froze. He recognized the music from when Angela had played it earlier in the apartment. The title of the song, *Come And Get Me,* was damned provocative. Jake just hoped to hell it didn't provoke more than what they anticipated. He was here to catch a killer, not fight a roomful of horny, out of control men.

He caught his first glimpse of Dark Angel. Holy hell, no wonder she'd had room for her costume in her purse. There was nothing to it. A miniscule black leather jacket covered what looked like a bra made of black fishnet. Even from this distance, he could see rose-colored nipples. She wore black bikini panties, black, thigh-high stockings and black boots. She finished off the look with short, black gloves. And for some unknown, freaky reason, those gloves called to him. The flash of a fantasy played in his mind—Angela wearing nothing but those gloves.

Long, raven-black hair fell like a silken waterfall over her creamy shoulders and rippled hypnotically with each sensual movement she made with the music. She grasped the pole, whirled, caressed and twisted around it, as if inviting a lover to her bed. Then she strutted away from the pole and faced the crowded room. The seductive expression on her face was that of a woman comfortable with her own sexuality. Her graceful movements invited intimacy, as if she were calling to her lover, aching for his touch.

A sharp pain in his left hand made him realize he was gripping the table so hard, the edge had cut into his palm. Relaxing his hold, Jake told his body to do the same. He had known he'd have a hard time with this—damned if he had known how hard.

Shifting uncomfortably in his chair, he ignored his physical response to the beautiful, sexy woman on stage, and tore his eyes away from her. The fact that he had watched four other women dance just as provocatively wearing even less clothing and hadn't been the least bit moved didn't matter…couldn't matter.

His gaze roamed the audience who seemed to be eating up the performance. Based on the ear-splitting wolf whistles, Dark Angel was a definite hit.

Even though the killer wouldn't come after her on stage, Jake carefully assessed each man. It was too dark to see faces but he had good enough night vision to observe body language. Not the best way to identify a killer, but seeing something 'off' could help pinpoint a possible suspect.

Tonight, on the way back to the apartment, would be the real test. Angela would walk home, seemingly alone and vulnerable. If the killer was watching tonight's performance and followed her, he would get the impression that Angela was easy prey. Jake looked forward to showing the bastard just how very alone she wasn't.

Shrill whistles brought his attention back to the stage. Jake cursed, softly, vehemently. Angela was hanging upside down from the pole, her long, beautiful legs twisting around the hard steel with a grace and strength that defied description. He had held her in his arms and felt the slenderness of her body but beneath the soft, silky skin was solid muscle. She made another twist, whirled and then landed back on her feet.

Once again, Jake forced his eyes away from the stage. He had two jobs, protecting Angela and catching a killer. Neither of those responsibilities involved staring like a salivating, sex-starved fiend. Unfortunately that was exactly how he felt.

As the song came to an end, the catcalls and whistles grew louder. Jake stood and moved easily between the tables, his eyes looking for any kind of a threat. No one even noticed his existence—he could be invisible. Their eyes were riveted to the stage. He dared a glance at the stage and jerked to a stop in the middle of the floor, his breath caught in his lungs. Other than the bikini panties and boots, Angela was completely nude. She'd even taken off those damn gloves.

Only by reminding himself that her protection was his number one priority was he able to look away. He turned and surveyed the crowd. All eyes were still focused on Dark Angel, seemingly mesmerized.

Just when he thought her first performance would end with no drama, a gorilla-sized man flung himself toward the stage, his giant hand within inches of grabbing Angela's ankle. As if it was a natural part of her performance, Angela gracefully stepped out of the man's reach. Roddy had warned them this might happen. It took every ounce of Jake's self-control to allow Justin Kelly to take care of the guy. The LCR operative grabbed the man by the collar, easily wrangling him back into his chair and then leaned over him for several seconds. Whatever Kelly had said worked because the man nodded and stayed seated.

The music ended and at last Angela's performance was over. Jake watched her as she left the stage, walking in that long-legged, loose-hipped sexy way she had, her strides unhurried and languid, full of that sexy confidence that had enthralled him from the first time he met her.

Dragging his attention away, he turned back to the audience. Anyone seem too extreme in their response? As another dancer was announced, he waited to see if anyone would walk out, thinking he'd found his next victim. No one moved.

It had been a long shot to believe the man could be targeted the first night, on the first performance. This might be a long, arduous op, taking weeks to complete. If tonight was any indication, Jake knew he was in for a tortuous time.

Angela sat alone in a corner of the dressing room. The other dancers seemed to recognize her need for isolation. Had they felt something similar their first time on stage? She had been so confident, sure that the experience wouldn't faze her. How wrong she had been.

Dancing in front of a small group in class, with a friendly, supportive instructor calling out directions and fellow classmates shouting encouraging words was a completely different experience from the real thing. The shouts had been lascivious and lewd, the encouragement had been vulgar, and the atmosphere had been anything but friendly.

Jake had been in that crowd. Of course she hadn't been able to see him but knowing he was in the audience had eased the feeling of aloneness as she'd stepped out onto the stage. That reassurance changed quickly. He had witnessed the crowd's reaction. She had known it wouldn't be easy for him but what she hadn't anticipated was how hard it would be for her, knowing he was watching it unfold.

Had he lost respect for her? Right now, friendship and respect were all they had. Would this mission she'd fought so hard for cost her that?

"Everything okay, ducky?"

Angela turned to see Monique, a tall, slender redhead whose stage name of Chili Pepper suited her.

"I'm fine. Thanks."

"First time?"

"Yes."

"You'll get used to it."

"Did you have problems the first time?"

"Oh yeah, cried for hours after. Told myself I wouldn't come back."

"Why did you?"

"Because I'm good and I make a lot of money. It got easier."

"How?"

She stared above Angela's head for several seconds and then said, "Distance. It's a job, not who I am. When I'm out there, I dance to the music, I think about a lover…" She shrugged and added, "Guess I go somewhere else."

That's what she had thought she could do too, but somehow that hadn't worked out. Not only had she been aware of the gawking, salacious eyes of the audience and Jake's overwhelming presence, she had been acutely conscious that one of those lust-filled gawkers might well be a serial killer. All of that was a bit much to handle for a first-time gig.

The sound of her cellphone pulled Angela back to the here and now. This was a job, nothing more. She had to keep that in mind. Thanking Monique for her advice, Angela reached for the phone she'd left at her dressing table.

"Hello?"

"You okay?"

Angela closed her eyes as Jake's deep, steadying voice soothed her. She wasn't alone in all of this. He was her partner and her friend.

"I'm fine." And because she was vain enough to want reassurance, she asked, "So how did I do?"

The long pause before he answered made her tense up. Had she done that badly?

"If you were any better, I would've had to jump up on the stage and carry you away."

She laughed, relieved to hear her nervousness hadn't shown through to ruin her performance. "To protect me from all the ravenous wolves in the audience?"

Another long pause. Angela could almost feel the electricity coming through the phone. When he answered, his voice was deeper, thicker. "The ravenous wolves had nothing to do with me wanting to carry you away."

"Oh." Amazing how one could become aroused in an instant. If Jake had been anywhere within touching distance, she would have been wrapped around him.

"You're not on for another hour. I think it would be best if you stay in the dressing room till your next set."

"Best for whom? You or me?"

His sigh exploded in her ear. "I'll see you after your performance. Stay with the plan."

Disappointed but not surprised, Angela answered coolly, "Will do."

She ended the call and dropped the phone onto the dresser. She shouldn't push him, she knew that. It didn't matter that he hadn't explained his reasons for not wanting to get involved. She knew his reasons. That should be enough to keep her away, but it wasn't.

# Chapter Nine

The night was too damn dark, almost eerie. Even the sky gave no relief of moonlight or stars. It was as if a black blanket covered the earth. The only light came from the soft glow of evenly spaced streetlights along the path. Cobblestones glistened beneath his feet while wisps of grey mist danced and spiraled around him like ghostly marionettes. Jake wasn't much of a horror movie buff but he'd seen enough as a kid to recognize a great atmosphere for a werewolf or vampire to pop out. Somehow, he'd rather deal with that kind of monster than the one they were hunting.

Angela, approximately seven yards ahead of him, was open, easy prey. Jake's focus was on his partner and their surroundings. She looked exactly as she needed to appear—alone, vulnerable, and completely unaware of any possible danger.

Kelly and Riley were out here, too. Both behind him, one to the right, the other to his left. He could neither see nor hear them but he felt their presence. If anything happened, they could respond in seconds.

Waiting for the killer to strike was the plan but damned if he liked it. Didn't matter that he could be at her side immediately if she needed him. It also didn't matter that she could easily take down a man without breaking a sweat. Angela in danger was hard to watch.

Her second performance had revealed no viable suspects. More than half of the men had been the ones who'd seen her first performance. None had acted unusual or caused warning bells.

But this was the real test. Angela walking home, alone, in the dark of night with a heavy mist turning every inanimate object into a threatening presence. Hell of it was, they still didn't know exactly how the killer made the grab. Did he take some of his victims out in the open? Or only from their homes? Did he deliver the roses and then attack? Maybe he made contact with them and they actually met before he took them.

As Jake had known all along—this was a fishing expedition and Angela was the bait.

She had barely even glanced his way when she'd left the club. He had expected nothing different since she could give no indication that they were more than mere acquaintances. Still he had detected an unusual aloofness in her attitude. Since he had known her, Angela had been an open book. He had never met anyone more open or emotionally available. Even after the hell of losing her entire family, she was willing to put her heart and emotions at risk. Having existed in shutdown mode for the last few years, her warmth and honesty jarred him, kicking at his wall of defenses unlike anything he'd ever experienced.

His gut told him something had changed tonight. Had she finally decided that he wasn't worth the trouble? Could he blame her? Hell no. He'd rebuffed her several times. Even with Angela's confidence, at some point he had figured she'd accept the reality of their relationship and let it go. So why the hell did he suddenly feel this massive regret?

He'd told Dylan he was a mixed-up son of a bitch. Sometimes he hated being right.

She could feel Jake's eyes even though she couldn't hear or see him. Just knowing he was there gave her reassurance. Even if he didn't want her in the way she wanted him, she knew he had her back.

Her normal confidence had returned, bringing with it a necessary and much-welcomed pragmaticism. Maybe it was the second performance that did it. She'd walked on to the stage, expecting to have the same experience as before, but everything felt different. She couldn't explain why. The audience had been just as lewd and crude as before. Men had thrown money at her feet, strange hands had slid paper money into her thigh-high stockings and her panties. And once again, many of those hands had tried to touch more. It should have made her feel just as vulnerable and exposed as the first time. Instead, she'd felt powerful. Maybe it was because she had taken the advice of the other dancers and danced only for one man. For her, that man was Jake.

She had imagined those dark blue eyes roaming over her body, his handsome face revealing desire and need. His hands clenched at his side to prevent himself from reaching for her. His entire body stiff and still, aching with all the delicious things he wanted to do to her. She had envisioned that after her performance, he would pull her to him and devour her mouth, then move down her body to the intense, needy throb between her legs aching for his mouth, his tongue.

Angela jerked herself back to reality of the moment. Dammit, she was on a job. A killer was out there and it was her responsibility to attract him. Looking distracted was supposed to be a ruse to make herself look vulnerable. It sure as heck wasn't supposed to be real.

She flipped her long hair off her right shoulder in a sexy, careless manner—most likely a useless gesture. If she hadn't attracted him while stripped to almost nothing, a little sexy hair play probably wasn't going to make a difference. Still, she felt the need to do something.

Stopping abruptly at a park bench, she propped her foot on the back and needlessly readjusted her thigh-high stockings. Her dress was already short and with her leg up like this, she revealed several more inches of skin.

A deep male voice growled in her ear, "What the hell are you doing?"

"Just adding enticement."

"And making it damn obvious you're wanting to attract attention," he snapped. "Get your ass moving again. Now."

Her first reaction was anger at his autocratic, abrupt tone. An instant later, she realized he was right. She dropped her foot and took off again. She wasn't out to attract every deviant, just one in particular. Jake was probably going to chew her out. She had made a rookie mistake and she was sure he would be happy to point that out. It didn't help to know that she deserved the reprimand.

She passed a young couple so wrapped up in each other they didn't notice her. The only other person she passed, an elderly man with a cane, barely glanced at her. She was almost at the apartment and though she knew attracting the killer her first night out hadn't been likely, she couldn't help but feel a little let down.

"Why are you slowing down? Keep moving."

Angela sped up and almost ran the last few steps to the apartment building. Inserting the key into the lock, she was inside in seconds. Not bothering to wait for the elevator, she sped up the stairs as if she were being chased. She heard the door slam behind her and knew that Jake had entered the building.

Racing down the hallway, she stopped at her door and then looked behind her. Jake wasn't there. Where was he? He had come in right after her. Hadn't he? Where had—

A large hand covered her mouth as a long, muscular arm snaked around her torso pressing her against a hard male body. "If I had been the killer, you'd already be drugged and I'd be taking you away."

The familiar voice growling in her ear jump-started a thousand emotions at once. Fear, frustration, anger, desire, need and so many more feelings culminated into an explosive reaction. Angela waited until he had loosened his hold and then acted in one smooth, continuous attack. She bit the hand covering her mouth, slammed her head back against him, then whirled and gave him a one-two punch, one in the face, the other in the gut.

It all happened so quickly, she barely let herself think of the consequences. It was when she saw the blood that she realized she'd gone too far. Jake was bent double, holding his stomach while blood poured from his nose.

Cursing herself, she quickly opened her apartment door and ran to the bathroom for towels. In seconds she was back. Jake had apparently regained his breath.

He was inside the apartment, leaning against the closed door and holding his nose to prevent more blood loss.

Remorse filling her, she held out the towel to him and whispered, "I'm so sorry. I don't know what came over me. I never—"

Jake shook his head as he took the towel and held it to his face. "Don't you dare apologize. You did exactly what you should have done. I deserved that for scaring you. My only criticism is that you should never have let me sneak up on you in the first place. You counted on me being behind you and you hesitated. Don't hesitate. The instant you feel threatened, you act."

"Yes, but I knew it was you when I did that."

Though his face was half covered with the towel, she could see that he was smiling. "Yeah, you were pissed. And I don't blame you. If anyone did that to me, I would have reacted the same way."

"Why didn't you stop me?"

"For one thing, I think you underestimate your skill. You move damn fast."

"And the other thing?"

He shrugged and moved further into the room. "I deserved the hit."

"Maybe so, but I could have held back on the punch."

"No, don't ever hold back. You can always apologize later if you made a mistake. But when someone grabs you from behind, you have every right to react the way you did."

"How bad is it?"

He lowered the towel and Angela wanted to cry. The lower half of his face was a bloody mess.

Whirling around, she ran to the bathroom again, dampened a washcloth and turned. Jake was standing behind her.

She put the lid down on the toilet and said, "Sit down and let me see how bad it is."

Jake knew this wasn't a good idea but he did it anyway. Apparently tonight was all about bad ideas. Trying to teach Angela a lesson in the midst of an op had been damned stupid. Either he trusted her or he didn't. Never one to lie to himself, he knew exactly why he'd done it. And it had nothing to do with trust. He had wanted an excuse to wrap his arms around her and feel her against him. He deserved what he got.

Angela leaned closer and began to wipe the blood from his face, her expression both anxious and tender. The temptation to pull her closer and kiss the small worry wrinkle on her forehead had him clenching his hands. The knowledge that she wouldn't deny him made his need all the more potent. He drew in a sharp breath.

She stepped back. "What's wrong? Does it hurt that much? Do you think your nose is broken?"

Grateful that she'd stepped out of his reach, he latched onto an excuse. "Actually I think it's my hand."

They both looked down at his hand and Angela gasped. A perfect imprint of her teeth covered the back of his hand. "Oh Jake, I'm so—"

"We've been through this before. Don't apologize."

"Did I break the skin?"

"I don't think so."

"Let me go get some ice for your nose and your hand. I'll be right back."

The instant she left the room, Jake stood and returned to the living room. The bathroom was too small for the both of them.

She came from the kitchen, a towel filled with ice in her hand, and then stopped abruptly when she saw him.

"I'd better get into my apartment or this entire op is going to be a bust."

"You're right. If he's watching me already, he needs to think I live alone."

Jake turned to the door that led to his apartment. One of the reasons they'd rented in this particular apartment building was this unique feature. The former owner of the building had moved his parents into an apartment next to his own. He had wanted access to the apartment without having to walk out into the hallway so he had installed a door between them. The feature was perfect for this op since it would appear that Angela lived in the apartment alone but Jake could get to her immediately if need be.

He opened the door and then turned. "You did well tonight."

"You mean the stripping part or the beating the hell out of you part?"

Forcing his mind away from the provocative image of Angela on stage, he said gruffly, "Both. But the little show you gave on the way home could have destroyed the whole op. Don't do that again."

Instead of hurt or anger, he saw only acceptance. "You're right, it was stupid of me."

On top of being one of the most beautiful women he'd ever known, why did she have to be so damned nice, too?

A stiff nod was the best he could manage as he went into his apartment and closed the door behind him. Leaning back against it, he ground his teeth until they hurt. Never in his life had he wanted a woman more. Even in the throes of young love when he'd first met Teresa couldn't compare.

After Teresa's death, Jake had existed in a vacuum. No one, not even his parents, had been able to penetrate the wall he had erected around himself. Then came the trials of all the bastards who'd chosen money over integrity and had been responsible for Teresa's and another woman's death. Cold fury had sustained him then. It wasn't until the last fucker was sentenced to life that he felt he could breath. And when he had taken that first breath, he realized he had to get away from everything.

Taking the life insurance money from Teresa's death, he had embarked on a journey. He hadn't known where he was going or what he was looking for... he had just known he couldn't be the same man or live in the same place where his life had exploded. His travels had taken him all over the world and in many of those places, he had been attracted to one woman or another. He had dated several and even had sex with a few of them. Not one of them had made him feel the way Angela did.

Jake wasn't much of a believer in fate but he had wondered if he'd somehow been led to that bar the day he had broken up LCR's sting and found himself a new job. And now, he had found a woman who made him feel again. Angela was breaking through every barrier he'd built. And every damn time he patched the wall up, she found a way to crack it once more.

No. He could not do this. He'd been there, done that, and couldn't survive the pain again.

Question was, how to fight every instinct inside him telling him to dive into the deepest end of the ocean where emotions and feelings swirled like a whirlpool, just waiting to suck him in and devour him?

He didn't know the answer. He only knew that Angela was his Achilles heel. But unlike the Greek warrior who was eventually destroyed because of his one vulnerability, Jake was determined to hide his own until it no longer existed. He refused to believe it was too late.

# Chapter Ten

Wolf whistles and catcalls heralded the closing moments of Luscious Lucy's act. Raucous shouts of praise intermingled with loud, lewd remarks. The audience was definitely wound up tonight.

Angela stood at the entrance to the stage, just out of sight. She'd been told that two different bachelor parties were in the audience. From the sound of it, both parties had imbibed more than their share of alcohol.

This was her fifth night of dancing. Each one had gotten progressively easier. The other dancers had been enormously supportive and their advice of going to another place in her mind or dancing for one man only had helped. Now, when she strutted out on to the stage, Jake was first and foremost in her mind. She heard the music but other distractions like whistles and crude remarks were greatly diminished. The fingers and hands that tried to grope her when they slid money into her clothing were a little harder to ignore. During those times, her teeth were grinding behind her smile. No one had complained that her smile was fake—her smile wasn't what they were looking at anyway.

She had even managed to forget she was dancing to attract a killer. He wasn't going to come after her on stage so she was able to be herself and dance the way she wanted and for the man she wanted.

In a way, this had been her communication with Jake this week. Since that first night when she had busted his nose, he'd been professional but distant. She knew it wasn't that he was holding a grudge. He was simply acting as her partner—which was exactly as he should act. That didn't prevent her from wanting more.

Now, as Lucy exited on the left side of the stage and Dark Angel's music started up, Angela focused on Jake—all the things she wanted to tell him, all the ways she wanted to love him. With him firmly in her mind, she glided on to the stage, her body swaying sensuously. She let the music take over. The size of the stage made it impossible for her to close her eyes for any length of time. The last thing she needed to do was fall into the audience. But she had learned that half-closed eyes worked just as well, allowing her to dismiss the dozens of eyes watching her and picturing only one set, hot with desire, filled with need and love as they roamed up and down her body.

Grabbing the pole, she swung effortlessly around, landed gracefully on her feet, then stepped back and looked up at it. In the place of a steel silver pole, stood a tall, sexy man with a square jaw, sensuous male lips, a noble Roman-like nose and piercing blue eyes. Yes, this was the man she wanted and loved.

Jake's image before her, Angela began to dance in earnest.

It had been the week from hell and was only getting worse. Jake leaned against the bar, his pose relaxed and indolent. He hoped he looked like a semi-bored owner of a strip joint. What was going on inside him had nothing to do with boredom and everything to do with going quietly insane.

Every night he had watched Angela come out on stage and each time she did, he could swear the temperature in the room increased by twenty degrees. Even though he watched the audience most of the time, he felt the need to check her on stage occasionally to make sure she was okay.

Mocking laughter sounded in his mind. Checking to make sure she was okay? Yeah, right. If he wasn't looking for a sadistic killer in the crowd, Jake knew he would've already gone up on stage and carried Angela away. In between bouts of lust that had him grinding his teeth to control, he had wanted to knock the hell out of some of the men because of their crude comments.

Day five of the op and nothing had happened. Not once had he detected anyone following Angela to her apartment. And even while she was on stage, the appearance and attitude of the audience was lascivious but not especially threatening.

Shea, Eden and Sabrina were working as waitresses in the other three sections the killer liked to roam and had reported the same negative results. Even though five days was a relatively short period of time, and attracting the killer so soon wasn't necessarily realistic, Jake had hoped for a quick resolution.

The shouts increased to a fever pitch, drawing Jake's eyes back to the stage where Angela was suspended upside down on the pole. And then, defying gravity, she spread her legs for mid-air splits. Sweat popped on Jake's forehead.

Tearing his gaze away, his eyes roamed the audience once more. The crowd was rowdier than usual. Two bachelor parties of a couple dozen men sat close to the stage, and the more acrobatics Angela performed with that damned pole, the louder they shouted. It was his and Kelly's job to anticipate trouble. Something in his gut told him that was going to happen tonight.

Without any seeming haste, Jake eased away from the bar and weaved his way toward the stage. He noticed Kelly was doing the same thing. Just as he reached the table where one of the bachelor parties was seated, a drunken young man threw himself onto the stage. At the same time, another man on the other side of the stage did the same thing. They were double-teaming, probably hoping that at least one of them would get away with grabbing Dark Angel.

Even though he wasn't the bouncer, Jake didn't hesitate to intervene. Just as a giant hand reached for Angela's ankle, Jake grabbed the back of the guy's waistband and hauled him off the stage. He noticed that Kelly was doing the same thing with the other man.

Whirling the guy around, Jake shoved him down into a chair and looked straight into his glazed eyes. "You try that again and I'll personally make sure you're drinking food through a straw for the next month." Jake waited a beat and then said, "Got that?"

Jake read the man's lips as he mumbled an apology. Releasing the guy's shoulders, Jake looked up at Angela. Hell, she hadn't missed a step. She was once again whirling upside down on the pole.

He checked out Kelly and noted he'd seated the other drunk. Making a sweeping glance around the audience, his eyes caught a glimpse of a shadow lurking in the doorway. Not wanting to draw attention to himself, Jake made his way toward the door. In seconds, the shadow was gone, leaving Jake wondering if he had imagined it. The light was so damn dim, was he seeing shadows where there weren't any?

Deciding to make sure, he walked out the door and looked up and down the street. There were plenty of people milling around on the sidewalk...none looked suspicious. Shrugging, Jake went back inside. Dark Angel had finished her set and left the stage. He blew out a relieved sigh, glad that the small drama was over at least for a while.

He returned to his post at the bar but found himself looking back frequently at the door. Something about the shadow bothered him. Had Dark Angel finally attracted the killer or was he being extra paranoid because of the adrenaline rush? Trusting his gut, he made a mental note to be hyper-vigilant while following Angela tonight.

Mired in disappointment and discontent, he roamed the streets of London. His newest acquisition hadn't brought him the peace he sought. He had hoped her differences would ease the roaring beast within him. Something about her had called to him and he had taken her against his own advice. Now he was filled with regret.

She was at his home, locked securely away. In his earlier days, he had made their home his own, believing that keeping them in their own environment added a bit more vitality to his activities. Their homes were places associated with security and safety. To be held hostage in your home gave a little extra emotional pain, which always improved a performance. Sometimes he'd watch their expressions and secretly laugh at the hope he saw in their faces. They were thinking that once their part was over, he'd leave them there, allowing them to get back to their safe, mundane world. Then, as each act became increasingly uncomfortable for them, he'd see that hope dwindling away like the slow drip of a faucet. The instant he saw the hope completely gone, he would revel in his power. Hope was a human condition—a failing. When it disappeared, perfection was almost complete.

When he began his activities in London, performing in their homes hadn't been necessary. His own grand mansion provided all the accoutrements necessary. And when it was time for them to leave, he'd had plenty of interesting places to play out their swan song.

Was there a point to holding on to this blonde-haired, green-eyed person? Was he keeping her out of stubbornness or a petty indulgence? She was just so different from all the others he hadn't even embarked on her training. Should he discard her and find someone more suitable?

At that thought, he felt resistance. He had learned to listen to his instincts. Perhaps his muse was leading him in a different direction. There was a reason he had chosen her, a reason she was different. He just didn't know why yet. Once he did, he was sure he would be back to his old self.

While he waited for that insight to appear, he would continue to hunt. His home was a fortress. She would be perfectly safe there. Nestled within a small community outside the city, no one would ever suspect such a staid, unassuming mansion was home to some of the most delightful performances ever created—such a pity he couldn't share those with everyone. That was the biggest reason he had to make their last performance so memorable. The world had to see what they had been missing.

Despite the convenience of being close to home, he would soon have to change his hunting grounds. He wasn't stupid. While he looked for his next treasure, others were hunting him.

He'd read numerous reports about his activities. Suppositions of why he did what he did. Everyone seemed to have a theory and none of them were right. He was in equal parts amused and insulted by their prosaic ideas. How dare they try to pigeonhole his genius into some sort of mundane explanation! The instant his methods were targeted, he changed his role. He was a chameleon, able to change with almost no effort. He had limitless talent, which was the very reason he had eluded authorities for years. They believed he had only begun a year ago. What imbeciles. Did they not realize this kind of genius took years to perfect?

The time had come to abandon London. Only one question remained. Would he discover the reason he'd taken his newest gem before he had to leave? If not, should he discard her or allow her to travel with him?

Crossing the street, engrossed in the possible problems involved in traveling with an unwilling companion, he paid little attention to his location until the titillating words of a song hit his ears. *"Come and get me. I know you want me. I'm yours for the taking. Come on…come on…come on. Come on, baby, come and get me."*

He jerked to a stop and gazed around. Though he had yet to acquire anything from this particular establishment, the surrounding area was one of his favorites to roam. Up and down the street, on both sides, were delicious places to prowl in hopes of finding the combination he required. Beauty and talent were hard to come by these days. Too many women relied on their looks alone. Beauty could only get one so far. That was the reason he'd had to try out so many.

The song continued, the words enticing him to investigate. He took three steps backward and peered into the dimly lit club. He'd been inside a couple of times…nothing had ever called to him before. But now he was enthralled as he listened to a song that spoke volumes about his needs, almost as if she were talking directly to him.

As he entered Club Drago, his heart pounded with exhilaration and triumph. Even when he hadn't been consciously looking for her, she had found him with her music. Happiness drenched his soul as he looked upon his future. She was perfect in every way…exactly as he'd always dreamed.

He watched in awe as she danced for him and no one else. Her exquisite body called to him as the song continued, telling him to take her, that she was meant for him. She undulated, twisted and swayed, as seductive as a siren. A temptress like none other. This was the one. Within the depths of his soul, he knew she was meant for him—wanted to be with him.

A disruption drew his attention away. Two unruly men were trying to touch what was his. Fury enveloped him. She was meant for him and no other. Thankfully, two large bouncers dispatched them quickly. Relieved, he turned his rapt gaze back to the mesmerizing creature on stage.

When the music ended, he gasped out a rush of air, unaware that he had been holding his breath. Temptation warred with practicality. He wanted her now, immediately. Thankfully his rational side took control. Just because she called out to him didn't mean others would understand their connection. Wearing only black panties and black boots, she turned and pranced off the stage. An ache tore at his heart as he watched her disappear from his view.

Soon she would perform for him in private. He would get to know her, learn her ways and then, if she were truly as talented as she seemed, Dark Angel would become his for eternity.

# Chapter Eleven

"Good show tonight, Love. You've really hit your stride."

Angela dressed, smiling her thanks as another compliment came her way. Ten performances in five days and she had definitely hit her stride. She was also beyond exhausted.

Tomorrow, when all the other regulars took off, she would perform again. She had never considered the physical toll of dancing twice a night. She had a feeling her weariness came from a combination of things. It was both mentally and physically exhausting to dance and strip in a roomful of strangers. Though she had been able to separate herself somewhat from the audience, she was still aware of them. Added to that was the knowledge that one of them might well be a serial killer and that should be enough for anyone. But there was more. Jake. Dancing for him gave her an opportunity to show him her feelings but what good did that do, really? He was looking for a killer, not an opportunity to get turned on.

Having Riley and Justin in the club actually added a bit of comfort, lessening the stress. Even though they had no interaction with each other, she saw them every night, going about performing their undercover jobs. Just knowing they were in the club made her feel less alone.

Since that first night, they had established a schedule of sorts. After her last performance, she would leave the club. She never deviated from the routine knowing that if the killer was watching, a different behavior might deter him.

Walking late at night, seemingly alone, on the streets of London, one would think something interesting or odd would happen. So far, the only unusual event had been two nights ago when an owl had swooped out of the sky into her path, startling her. Other than that, her lonely sojourn back to her apartment was done in relative peace.

Since it was suspected that the killer stalked his victims for days before abducting them, she had developed daytime habits as well. A solo breakfast at a nearby restaurant, short shopping jaunts to various stores, another solo restaurant meal for lunch, and then she would return to her apartment. If he were out there watching her, he would see that she had little social life or interaction with others. Hopefully this behavior was to his liking.

An hour before she was to leave for the club, Jake would knock softly and politely on the mutual door they shared between his apartment and hers. She had come to both look forward to and dread the visit. Being with him was a reminder that this was all he wanted from her—a professional relationship. But it was also an opportunity to be with him so she took what she could get.

Pulling the earbud from her purse, she inserted it into her ear. And like clockwork, she heard his voice. "You there?"

"Yes," she answered softly.

"Thought I saw someone lurking about tonight. Couldn't get a good look though. Might've been nothing but be extra aware, just in case."

A shiver of unease zipped up her spine. "Okay."

"It's almost eleven. I'll be at my usual place."

She shrugged into her thick coat, grabbed her purse and headed toward the back entrance. All employees used this entrance, which she and Jake feared put her at a disadvantage of not being seen. It was a hidden door and from the outside one couldn't even tell it was a door. However, if she used a different exit, that might look suspicious. The last thing they needed was the killer to suspect she was anything other than a typical hard-working woman, just as his other victims had been.

She went through the door and was instantly cold. Mother Nature had the entire city in her frozen grip. For the past week the temperatures had hovered in the mid-twenties in the daytime and mid-teens at night. Weather reports predicted single digits tonight.

Wrapping her arms around herself, she headed out of the alleyway toward the apartment, the even sounds of Jake's breathing in her ear her only comfort. After she left the busy street, her way home was a lonely, sinister path. An occasional horn from a ship pulling into the harbor or the burst of boisterous laughter from the district she'd just left were sounds that had become familiar.

Exhaustion wrapped around her like a wet, soggy blanket. Fatigue, along with Jake's warning, made the night seem more ominous than usual. She straightened her drooping shoulders and shook off her disquiet. When she got back to the apartment, she'd take a hot shower and—

The distant click of rapid footsteps rushed adrenaline through her veins. Before tonight, not once had she heard Jake or anyone else following her. That could only mean one thing. Someone, a stranger, was coming up behind her.

"I hear him." Jake voice was soft and calm in her ear. "You've slowed down a little. Just keep walking like normal. Ingram is up ahead of you, to your right. Kelly is behind me to my left. Someone is directly behind you. It's too damn dark to see where he is but just act natural."

Act natural? Her heart thudded with dread, her limbs felt weighted and awkward. It was as if she'd never had any kind of training. As if this wasn't her job. She took deep breaths to try to control the growing panic and whispered soundless reassurances to herself. Jake was with her, ready to pounce if this guy got too close. And Riley and Justin were nearby, too. They could be at her side in seconds. In the back of her mind, Angela acknowledged that Noah had been right. Training in a safe environment was different than being in the field. She couldn't imagine doing this alone, without a partner to watch her back.

"Sounds like he's to your left now."

Her steps sped up to match the rhythm of her heartbeat. She was like any other lone woman who heard a strange noise in the night. The need to escape was almost a compulsion.

"Okay, you're walking too fast now. Slow down a bit. Let's see if he'll catch up with you."

Breath puffed out in panicked spurts. Terror zipped up her spine. Every survival instinct within her told her to run. Was this it? Was she about to be attacked? Her mind went blank. She forgot every lesson she'd ever learned. What if Jake couldn't get to her in time? What if she couldn't see the killer coming?

"I think I see him. In the park, beneath that clump of trees. Don't look that way."

No sooner had he spoken when she felt a rush of air and something clipped her arm. Thrown off balance, Angela tried to catch herself and ended up sprawled face first onto the pavement.

She heard Jake's curses and more running feet. Ignoring the pain in her hand from where she'd tried to catch herself, she sprang to her feet and looked around wildly.

"Excuse me, Miss, are you all right?"

A small shriek escaped her as she turned to see a policeman a few feet away.

"Yes, I think so. I don't know what happened."

"I saw it all. Some kid came running toward you, then jumped up on a skateboard and swooped by you. It's a wonder he didn't knock you flat." He came closer and peered down at her. "Are you sure you're not hurt?"

Her teeth chattered, making it difficult to speak but she managed the words, "Yes, yes, I'm fine. Thanks."

"If you're really okay," Jake growled in her ear, "say the words, 'Thank you for your help, but I'm all right.' Otherwise I'm coming over."

"Thank you for your help but I'm all right." And she was, really she was. Other than a pounding heart, a throbbing hand, and the terrible, terrible knowledge that something was very wrong.

The policeman tipped his hat. "Best get home then. A cold night to be out and about."

She managed a whispered "Thank you" and turned to head to her apartment, her steps much quicker than before. Now that the excitement was over, her limbs were shaking with reaction. She dashed inside the building and ran up the stairway as if death itself was on her tail. Stopping in front of her apartment, she cursed as she gripped the keys in her left hand. She was shaking so badly, she was having difficulty inserting the key. Her right hand hung uselessly at her side.

"Angela, listen to me. Take slow, even breaths. You're fine."

For the first time, she realized that Jake had been saying those words repeatedly the entire time she'd been running.

Finally, at last, the key went in and she twisted the doorknob. Half a second later, she was inside and slamming the door closed. Leaning back against it, she drew in breaths as she tried to control the panic. As the terror slid away, something equally devastating was taking its place. How had she not seen this coming?

Between bursts of her heavy, sporadic breathing, she heard Jake enter the apartment next door. Seconds later, he came through the attached door and into the living room.

For the life of her she couldn't make her frozen limbs move. A disdainful voice inside her told her to straighten up, walk toward him, assure him she was fine. Laugh off the incident as a moment of slight panic and nothing more.

When she didn't move, the voice called her a coward. She couldn't deny the words. Pangs of disillusionment and disappointment were quickly swamping the fear. The astonishment on Jake's face confirmed her thoughts. Who would have thought that Angela Delvecchio was actually a paper tiger?

Jake carefully approached the terrified woman slumped against the door. Seeing the strong, confident Angela reduced to a shivering, frightened girl hurt him in ways he'd never expected.

Fearing she was still in the grips of panic, he stopped a foot away and bent his knees to get eye contact. Relieved to see recognition in them, he moved forward and gently drew her into his arms. "You're safe now. No one's going to hurt you. I promise."

With Angela, he had come to expect the unexpected. Never could he have been prepared for what came next. With a cry that sounded as mournful as a beaten animal, she buried her face against him and burst into tears.

So used to a sassy, in-your-face Angela, Jake began to panic himself. Had she been hurt and he hadn't seen it? Pulling away from her, he whispered urgently, "What's wrong? Are you hurt somewhere?"

When she kept her head down and continued to cry, he shook her gently. "Tell me what's wrong."

She answered brokenly, "I'm a big wuss."

Relief flooded through him. The urge to shake her again for scaring him was overwhelmed with the need to hold her and be grateful that she was unharmed. Just as he put his hands on her shoulders to pull her back into his arms, he noticed the hand she held at her side.

"Dammit, you are hurt."

Gingerly he lifted her right hand and hissed as he assessed the damage. Without a doubt it was sprained, possibly broken.

"Sweetheart, why didn't you tell me you were hurt?"

She stared at her hand as if it were a foreign object she'd never seen before. Shock was rapidly taking the place of the adrenaline overload from her scare. Moving carefully to keep from startling her, Jake scooped her into his arms, taking special care not to jar her hand.

In three strides he was at the couch where he placed her gently against the pillows. He turned and headed to the kitchen. Hot, sweet tea for the shock and then they were going to the hospital to get her hand x-rayed.

He glanced over his shoulder. She lay where he left her, the hollow, desolate look in her eyes worrying him more than the damage to her hand. He wanted to hold her and reassure her, but had a feeling doing that would be more for his benefit than hers. She had scared the hell out of him.

With quick efficiency, he poured water into a cup, dropped in a teabag and put it in the microwave. Not the proper British way to make a cup of tea but he was looking more for expediency than taste. The instant the bell dinged, he took the steaming cup, liberally added several spoonfuls of sugar and headed back to the couch where Angela lay, unmoving.

He set the cup on the coffee table and then pulled her to sit up. Propping her against his shoulder, he grabbed the cup and held it in front of her, allowing the steam to coat her face. "Take a sip."

Her lips parted and Jake held the rim of the cup to her mouth and tilted it slightly. When he heard her swallow, the tension in his muscles loosened. At least she was responding to his verbal commands. Now to get the hot soothing liquid and sugar boost flowing in her veins and hopefully get her talking.

They sat silently for a minute or more. The only sounds came from Angela's sipping and swallowing the hot beverage. He was glad to see color was returning to her face and the glassy look disappear from her eyes.

Noting the tea was almost gone, Jake lowered the cup. He was about to ask her if she wanted more when she expelled a gargantuan sigh. Her gaze locked on the cup he still held in his hand, she spoke softly, "For most of my adult life, I've wanted to be an LCR operative. I used to dream about rescuing people and how wonderful that must feel. The thrill of taking down bad guys, the satisfaction that came from saving victims… It's been my dream for so long. And now…"

Jake frowned. "And now, what?"

She snorted softly. "And now it's apparent that I'm not cut out for it."

"Don't be ridiculous. LCR operatives get scared just like everyone else. It was your first time. Don't be so hard on yourself."

Sad beyond measure, Angela shook her head. She appreciated Jake's words, especially since he hadn't wanted her on this job in the first place, but she now knew the truth. The smallest of scares and she'd folded like a defective chair. And that was how she felt—defective. She hadn't been able to function or think straight. If the skateboarder had been the killer, she would have shrieked like a banshee and probably gotten herself and even Jake killed.

The throbbing pain in her hand was nothing compared to the dull ache in her heart. It had taken only seconds for her dreams to be demolished.

"We need to get you to a hospital and have your hand checked out. Does it hurt?"

"A little…not much."

"Think you can manage to get to the car on your own?"

"Yes, but where are you going?"

"With you but we can't be seen together. We can't blow our cover."

Angela shook her head. "It doesn't matter anymore. I'm off the op."

The man beside her jerked as though he'd been burned. "What the hell are you talking about?"

"I'm not an active field operative anymore. I'm going back to my job as a researcher, that is, if Noah isn't too pissed at me."

When Jake pulled completely away from her and stood, Angela felt cold and lifeless as if he'd taken all the warmth and vitality with him. For several silent seconds he stood, looking down at her. Ashamed of her cowardice, she didn't raise her head.

"We'll discuss this later. Your hand is swelling rapidly. Let's go."

She had disappointed him—it was in his voice. She didn't blame him. There was no one more disappointed in her than she was in herself. Of all the scenarios she had envisioned about her first op, this hadn't been on her radar. Who would have thought something as innocuous as a kid on a skateboard could destroy her dream?

Feeling like a tired, lifeless creature, Angela grabbed her purse and went out the door, Jake following closely behind her. They had broken their cover—her part in the op was officially over. And now all she felt was empty and sad, much like she had when she lost her family. Jake, the man she loved and admired, walked by her side but never had she felt more bereft and alone.

# Chapter Twelve

Jake had felt helpless plenty of times in his life, but he usually had a clue how to fix things. Not this time.

The instant they'd gotten into the car, Angela had phoned McCall. The conversation had been short and one-sided. She had been calm but resolute as she told him she was no longer on the job.

The emotionless way she'd announced her decision must have stunned McCall. At the hospital, once the nurse had taken Angela into an exam room, Jake had called his boss. McCall's "What the hell happened?" wasn't a surprise. What struck him was the sadness he heard in the man's voice.

Quickly and succinctly, Jake described the evening's events. McCall had expelled a long, ragged breath. "Bring her back here when you can. She'll want to talk to Samara."

The LCR leader had ended the call with disturbing information. Another woman was missing. There was no seeming tie to the disappearances of the other women with the exception of a bouquet of red roses found in the woman's home. Neither a stripper nor a waitress, the missing woman worked at a small investment firm. Her home was in a different area of the city from where the other victims had lived. Plus, her physical characteristics had nothing in common with the killer's preferences. The only similarities were the roses and the fact that she had vanished without a trace. The police were tentatively treating her disappearance as related.

After talking with McCall, Jake debated his next move. Telling the others, Riley Ingram and Justin Kelly, that he and Angela were off the job felt too precipitous. He wanted to wait and talk to Angela again after she'd had a while to think about her decision. Just because she'd told McCall she was off the case didn't mean things couldn't be reversed. Why he was so concerned about changing her mind escaped him. Only a week ago, he would've been happy to hear she had decided against being an operative. Now, he wanted to convince her to stay the course.

Jake shoved his fingers through his hair. Hell, his thinking was as skewed as Angela's.

The door behind him opened. He whirled around and watched as she wandered into the room like a lost waif. And he knew why he wanted to change her mind. Before this incident, there had been a bright, unquenchable light in her eyes. The brightness was gone, leaving them dull and sad.

She held up a bandaged hand. "It's a slight sprain. No fractures. The doctor said it should be fine within a week or so."

"That's good news."

She grimaced a half smile. "I guess we can leave."

In silence they left the hospital, got in the car and headed back to the apartment. Jake searched for the right words—something he could tell her that would make her rethink the experience and realize her fear had been natural. The truth hit him between the eyes and with a sigh, he opened his mouth and did something rare. He began to talk about his past.

"I went into the Army gung-ho and clueless. Took to the training like a duck in water. Everything they asked of me, I was eager for the challenge and excelled in it. Ask me to shoot a target, I was dead-on. Drop me in the middle of wilderness with no equipment and I'd find my way home, no problem. Tell me to swim a mile in the ocean and then hike twenty miles just to capture a damn flag, I was all over it."

As he talked, Angela sat quietly, unmoving. He knew he had her attention because her body was stiff, as if she were holding her breath. Encouraged, he continued,

"Then came my orders. They were sending me to Afghanistan. I was going to fight, probably kill, and possibly be killed. It finally hit me that I was going to have to put all those skills I'd learned and excelled at to use. I was scared shitless."

Jake thought back about that time. Today he could smile at that too eager kid who enjoyed playing Army until it came time to man-up and actually do what he'd been trained to do.

"What did you do?"

Pleased at the question, he continued his story. "The night after I got my orders, I lay in my bunk and thought about all the things that could happen. The harder I thought about it, the more I panicked. The next day, I was headed to talk to my sergeant, ready to admit that I wasn't prepared. On the way, I passed by the chapel. I thought, 'What the heck? I'll go in and have a talk with the Big Guy before I give it all up.'

"The chaplain happened to be in his office as I passed by, and for whatever reason, maybe because I looked scared or probably because he'd seen the same thing in hundreds of other soldiers, he invited me inside. I sat down and let it spill. Every fear, every scenario my brain could come up with..."

They pulled into a parking space in front of the apartment complex and Jake paused to see if Angela would stay and listen. She didn't move.

"The chaplain listened while I poured out everything bubbling within me. When I was finished, I thought he'd probably tell me I was right to want to quit, that I would be doing my country a favor. Instead, he just nodded his head and said one simple sentence."

"What?"

"He told me that when it's time, God gives you the courage to do what you need to do." Jake shrugged. "He was right."

Several seconds of silence passed. Finally when he realized she wasn't going to ask any more questions, Jake opened his door. He was coming around the car to help her out when she got out on her own and said baldly, "The difference between you and me is that when it was time, you had the courage to follow through. I didn't."

Jake stood outside Angela's bedroom, unsure of his next move. He almost felt like that clueless kid again, struggling with the right thing to do and afraid of doing the wrong thing. What he wanted was to barge into the bedroom, force a confrontation, igniting her anger and that fiery spirit he admired. Seeing Angela so defeated tore at him like a jagged knife. Good judgment told him to let her be—the rest would do her good. Tomorrow, after a good night's sleep, she'd have a different perspective.

He turned the knob and pushed the door open. Good judgment be damned.

The sound of the shower from the bathroom should have stopped him. He was aware she took a shower every night after her performance. Dancing worked up a healthy sweat and she'd commented more than once that she smelled. Jake couldn't tell her that he loved the natural fragrance of her body. Admitting that would get them into a territory he was determined to avoid.

So why the hell was he headed where he was sure to find trouble?

He stopped at the entrance to the bathroom. Steam billowed from the shower but Angela stood in the middle of the room. The humid mist was so thick, he couldn't see her clearly. He waved to clear his vision and then froze. She was standing in the middle of the room, completely nude with the exception of those damn black boots. Unable to look away, his eyes roamed over her. Yes he saw her almost every night with little more on than what she was wearing now. This was different. The setting was intimate and if he reached out his hand, he'd be touching that soft-as-silk skin. From the tip of her long elegant feet to the top of her beautiful head, she was perfection. Impossibly long legs, slender hips, taut, flat stomach, perfect globes for breasts, slender, feminine shoulders, and a face both exotic and ethereal. It was as if every fantasy of the perfect woman had culminated into the making of Angela Delvecchio.

"I can't get my boots off."

While he'd been standing here, salivating like a teenager in the first throes of sexual arousal, she'd been working to remove her clothes to take a shower. Her injured hand prevented her from tugging the boots off. Never had he felt more like a heel.

"Sit on the edge of the tub. I'll pull them off."

When she complied, Jake went to his knees and lifted a booted foot. He told himself he was performing a service. Appreciating the view shouldn't be part of the equation. Yet in this position, how could he not look? She was smooth and hairless, everywhere. He knew about Brazilian waxes. Had heard they were painful. As a stripper, it made sense that she'd had the procedure done. Yet all he could think about was whether or not she'd been like that before this mission and what would she do if he leaned forward and tasted her sweet, moist flesh?

Swallowing hard, he tugged at her boot and removed it slowly, torturing himself as he exposed even more beautiful skin. One boot off and one to go, he glanced up at her face, sure that he would see the same need that was roaring through his bloodstream. Instead her eyes were closed and tears streamed down her face. Hell and damnation, enough with his inappropriate lust. She was suffering.

He removed the second boot, stood and pulled her to her feet. "Get in the shower." He grimaced at the thick, gruff command but was surprised he'd been able to speak at all.

"I'm not supposed to get my hand wet."

"I'll help you."

She turned and stepped over the rim of the tub. Jake adjusted the nozzle, and grabbed the sponge hanging from a hook on the wall. He poured fragrant liquid soap onto the sponge, recognizing the scent that drove him crazy every time she was near.

"I think I can manage almost everything with one hand but could you stay and prop me up?"

Rivulets of water streamed a caressing path over her shoulders and down her luscious curves. Mesmerized, all Jake could manage was a small grunt of agreement to her request. Then with great difficulty, he pulled the shower curtain closed, shutting out the delectable sight of her soapy body.

Holding her slender, elegant hand in his own, Jake closed his eyes and tortured himself as he imagined the scene behind the curtain. In his mind, her hand became his as he slowly caressed down her body, from soft, beautiful shoulders to her breasts. He swirled the sponge around each ivory globe and then trailed it down her flat stomach toward the soft mound between her legs. His hand moved between her legs and then the sponge was gone. His fingers touched unbelievably hot, smooth flesh and—

"Jake?"

Pulling himself out of his fantasy, Jake managed a thick, raspy, "Yeah?"

"Could you help me wash my hair?"

*Oh hell.*

Feeling both fragile and powerful at once was an odd combination. She was so disappointed in herself because of her cowardice, a part of her wanted to bury her head beneath the bedcovers and forget reality. But seeing the desire in Jake's eyes made her feel stronger, more secure. And though she had known Jake was attracted to her, the need she'd seen in his eyes made her realize just how much he wanted her.

And yet, he had done nothing more than look. If she made any advances to him, would that shut him down? His rejection, especially tonight, wasn't something she was willing to risk. If he turned down her offer, she'd shatter into a billion pieces right in front of him.

She finished her shower, albeit a little awkwardly. How odd to have Jake outside the shower curtain holding her hand. The act was gentlemanly and courteous but also amazingly erotic. The connection of him holding one of her hands while her other one glided over her body was uniquely arousing. Every place she touched, she imagined it was Jake's hand instead of her own.

Now came the biggest test as she waited for him to respond to her request to help her wash her hair. Though she had been aware of the tenseness of his body outside the curtain, when she asked the question, he went board stiff. Would he say no?

The curtain opened and Jake stood there. If she had thought she saw desire before, it was nothing like what he was experiencing now. Blue fire blazed in his eyes, dark, wicked…knowing.

Angela stood, mesmerized.

He picked up her shampoo bottle. "I'll pour the shampoo in your hand and then help you massage it in."

The hoarse growling was barely recognizable as Jake. She did as he asked and then he put her injured hand against the wall, outside the shower. "This will go faster if I can use both of my hands. Keep your hand here."

When she complied, he said, "Now, bend your head."

What followed was one of the most erotic moments of her life. Jake's big, strong hands, along with her much smaller one lathered her hair into a soapy mass of bubbles and foam. Her eyes closed, she swallowed moans of arousal as strong fingers massaged her scalp and the back of her neck. Never had she realized the correlation between her head and her sex. For every strong press of his fingers, a corresponding throb occurred between her legs.

"Rinse."

Though water gushed over her, she had no problem hearing the husky thickness of his tone.

Standing beneath the spray, she allowed Jake to rinse the soap from her hair. It took an enormous amount of self-control for her not to grab his hand and lead him to other, hidden places aching for his touch.

At last the soap was gone. The water stopped abruptly as Jake turned off the faucet. Angela opened her eyes and watched in agony as Jake turned away. Was he walking out, just leaving her like this?

A large towel covered her head and Angela smiled beneath it as Jake dried her hair. Then, as if it was just another day at the office, he efficiently and effectively dried her entire body.

"Let's get you out of there before you get a chill."

He helped her out of the shower and then she stood in the middle of the bathroom, stark naked, and waited for his next move. Yes, she knew she could leave and go throw some clothes on. She also knew she could touch him and probably get what she'd wanted almost from the moment she met him. She did neither—this was Jake's call.

Every particle of Jake's body felt like it was on the cusp of explosion. Cupping her face with his hands, he stared down into a dark velvet gaze filled with need. Angela had never closed herself off from him and she wasn't now. Expressive, beautiful eyes told him she was his for the taking. And God help him, he was going to take all she could give.

He watched her eyes widen as he lowered his head. Before he pressed his mouth to hers, he whispered softly, "You're sure?"

At her soft response of "With everything that I am" Jake was lost. The instant his lips covered hers, he was engulfed in an erotic burning haze. Sweeter than any delicacy he'd ever tasted, her mouth offered sensual delights he had never imagined.

He pulled away from her soft, luscious lips and then closed his mouth over her breast, sucking deeply, his tongue flattened against her nipple as he pulled at her. The breathy, gasps coming from Angela urged him on. But he needed more. With a growling "Hold on" he cupped her beautiful ass in his hands, lifted her and headed to the bedroom.

Following his orders perfectly, she wrapped her legs around his waist and held tight. Jake could hear words of caution and reprimands coming at him from various sources in his head. He shut them down. He had dreamed about this forever… had wanted Angela from the moment he met her. She had made no secrets of her desire for him. They were two consenting adults performing an act as old as time. It was nothing more than that.

The instant the back of her legs hit the bed, Jake pushed her all the way onto the bed and then followed her down. His mouth became a marauder as he delved into every valley and shadow on her silken body. Starting at her long, elegant neck, he caressed with his hands and his tongue, leaving a trail of wet kisses as he glided to her breasts where he once more tasted each one. With great reluctance, he lifted his mouth and stared down at them. The soft glow of moonlight from the bedroom window highlighted gleaming mounds of perfection.

About to go back for another taste, she arched slightly, brushing her body up against him, reminding him he had even more treasures to taste. Lowering his head again, he kissed and licked her stomach and followed a slow, delicious path to her long legs. Trailing kisses down one leg, he stopped at the bottom, picked up her foot and licked from heel to the top of her toes. Looking up to see what kind of effect that had on her, he became lost in the dark sensuality of her eyes where every emotion was revealed to him—acceptance, arousal and desire. All the things he needed to see.

Taking her other foot, he performed the same taste test and then, still holding her foot in his hand, he leaned forward, bending her leg as he went. And there she was, exposed and open for him. She arched toward him in blatant invitation. With a deep growl of approval, Jake dipped his head. Pausing at her entrance, he breathed in the musky scent of arousal. Never had he smelled anything sweeter. Spreading the folds of her sex, his tongue licked in a long, deliberate swipe. Her hitching breath made him smile. Yes, they both wanted it. This time he went deep, thrusting all the way inside her. Hot moisture hit his tongue as he delved over and over again. Angela's fingers weaved into his hair, her hands pressed him deeper between her legs. Hell, he could spend a lifetime eating her. Her breath hitched higher and when climax hit, she tightened like the taut string of a musical instrument, her body arching upward toward his greedy mouth. Grabbing her hips to still her movements, his tongue delved as deep as he could go as he let her ride his mouth to fulfillment.

Breathless and panting as if she'd just run a marathon in a matter of minutes, Angela wound down from the most deliciously exquisite orgasm of her life. Jake's head was still between her legs, gently lapping. Wanting to give him the same kind of pleasure, she cupped his jaw in her hand and whispered, "Jake, let me taste you, too."

She had a flash of fear that regret would set in and he'd leave her without letting her have the same luxury of delighting in his body. That fear was obliterated when he sprang to his feet and stripped with impressive speed and no finesse.

She laughed softly. "It's a good thing you're not a stripper by trade. The show would be over before it started. You are—" She broke off on a gasp. He was…there was no other word for it…he was beautiful. She had never even seen him without a shirt, which was probably a good thing because she would have been all over him. Every inch of his body was steel encased in smooth, hard silk.

She stretched out her hand and was instantly mesmerized by the feel of him beneath her fingers. He dropped down beside her and then did something no other lover had ever allowed her to do. He sprawled out before her and gave her total access to his body, allowing her to touch him anywhere, everywhere. Her hands glided over him as if he was a piece of fine art and she was a connoisseur. Her fingers trembled as they roamed over the steel hard muscles of his shoulders and chest. The slight furring in the middle of his chest was a delight to touch, the hair coarse and silky at once. She swirled a fingertip around a copper nipple and smiled when it sprang up hard, as if eager for attention.

Trailing her hand down his torso, she explored the hard planes of his abdomen. Her gaze lowered and despite her knowledge that big men often had big parts, she couldn't prevent the gasp at his size. Without thought of consequences, her only desire was to taste the long, hard length, she opened her mouth and took the head into her mouth.

Jake drew in a sharp breath and pulled away.

She looked up at him. "What's wrong?"

"Not a damn thing. Just didn't expect that."

"Can I have more…now that you know?"

His laughter was a short bark. "Baby, you can have as much as you want."

She smiled. "I don't think I can handle as much as I want." Lowering her head again, she took him back into her mouth and to her throat, testing exactly how much she could take. When he reached her throat, she pulled away to keep from gagging, then tried again. The sounds coming from Jake told her he approved. She reveled in his taste, in the sheer loveliness of being able to give him pleasure.

Seconds later, Jake pushed her away and grabbed her shoulders. Before she could ask him why, he had flipped her onto her back and was devouring her mouth like a starving man. Angela wrapped her arms around him and opened her legs wider, allowing Jake to settle between them. And with one hard, driving thrust, he pushed deep inside her.

Angela met each thrust with a counterpoint arch of her body. In perfect rhythm, as if they had synchronized and planned this sexual dance, their bodies writhed and twisted. Coupled with the need for fulfillment was the desire to give each other everything they had. For every groan from Jake, Angela gave a moaning approval of her own. In beautiful sexual connectivity, they took what they wanted and gave all that was asked.

He stiffened and she knew he was close. Grabbing his hips, she arched up and pushed him even deeper, igniting her own explosive climax. On a wail of ecstasy, release washed over and in that splendid moment of sweetness, Angela knew that her life would never be the same.

# Chapter Thirteen

Cocooned in a hard, warm embrace, Angela snuggled against Jake's chest and allowed herself the fantasy of forgetfulness and peace. She had never expected to be here with him like this. What they had just experienced was something she wanted to hold on to for as long as possible.

She pressed a lazy kiss to his chest and sighed. "I don't think I've ever been this relaxed."

"Me either." He released a sigh. "It's a little late to talk about it, but I didn't use protection and I—"

"Not to worry. I'm covered." She peeked up at him. "Healthy, too."

He dropped a kiss on her nose. "Me too."

"Good."

His arms tightened around her and they lay in perfect quietness for several more seconds. And then Jake broke the silence and said, "Tell me about your family. Are you more like your father or your mother?"

Loving the rumble of his voice beneath her ear, she wiggled deeper into his arms. "One of mama's favorite sayings was: 'I swear, Angela, you're just like your papa.' "

"You weren't like your mother?"

Angela laughed. "Oh yes, very much so. In fact, my father would always counter with, 'No, Elena, she's just like you.' "

Grateful for the opportunity to share the memories of her loved ones with Jake, she continued, "My family was wonderfully unique but I guess a typical one, too. We had our disagreements. My father wanted my brother to study architecture but Max wanted to be a painter. He was an amazing artist. From the time he could walk, he knew exactly what he wanted to do with his life. That didn't prevent my parents, especially Papa, from trying to influence him. He never budged." Her voice held a wealth of sadness as she added, "He was on his way to fulfilling his dreams."

Dropping a comforting kiss to her head, he said, "And your sister, Chloe, what was she like?"

Her eyes closed to prevent the tears, she said, "Like a peaceful river."

"What do you mean?"

Angela shrugged, unsure if she could do justice to her sweet little sister. "She just had a way about her that was calming. She possessed a maturity far beyond her age. My parents and brother had a tendency toward drama, often overreacting to even the most mundane events. Chloe was even-keeled and serene. She took things in stride and gave great advice."

Humor in his voice, he said, "So it was just your brother and parents who were dramatic?"

Angela laughed. "Okay, me too."

"And Chloe gave great advice. She give you any?"

"Absolutely. In fact, Chloe was the only one in my family who knew I worked for LCR. I never told my parents or my brother because I knew how they would react. And Noah feared they could be targeted if any of his enemies knew, so I kept it to myself."

"But not Chloe?"

"She didn't know for a long time but one day we were talking about our dreams for the future. Chloe wanted to be a teacher, like Papa. She used to play schoolhouse with her friends…she was always the teacher. Anyway, she asked me what I wanted to do."

"And you told her you wanted to be an LCR operative?"

Pain seared her heart and tears threatened again…that dream was dead. Chloe would be so disappointed in her. Unable to verbalize her answer, Angela nodded.

"And what was her reaction?"

"She was surprised but pleased, too. I think she saw me as some kind of superhero." She snorted softly. "Little did she know."

As if she hadn't just touched on a painful subject, Jake said, "And your parents? What were they like?"

"Mama was sweet, wise, and self sacrificing. Papa was temperamental, loving, and had a great sense of humor.

"To Mama, family was the most important thing. Despite the fact that she didn't want to leave the States and come to Paris to live, she did it for my father and our family. I was only ten but I remember how sad she looked when we arrived, as if she'd lost her best friend. Papa tried to make it better for her, reassuring her that she would soon love France as much as she loved America. I don't think she ever did but she adjusted eventually. And she did whatever she could to make sure her children never forgot that part of their heritage."

"How'd she do that?"

"Family dinners were a big thing for the Delvecchio's. You could miss breakfast and lunch but you never missed dinnertime. It was served promptly at six o'clock. If you were late, you had to pay a price."

"Like what?"

"Hmm. Like naming the past presidents of the U.S. Sometimes you could get by with just naming the fifty states, reciting the Preamble to the Constitution or the Pledge of Allegiance. If you were really late, it was the Gettysburg Address or you'd have to sing the national anthem." She giggled as she added, "We all suffered when that happened since not one of us could carry a tune."

She remembered one particularly controversial mealtime. "Papa was an educator and was usually all for such discipline but one day he was fifteen minutes late and Mama made him pay dearly for it. He had to name the fifty states."

"That doesn't seem that hard."

"It is when you have to name them in date order of when they became a state."

"Hell, that is harsh."

"Yes, he wasn't too pleased but she had made his favorite meal, so he had incentive."

Jake chuckled. "Your family was unique."

"That they were. I miss them so much." Encouraged by the intimacy they'd shared, as well as his questions about her family, she said, "What about yours? What's your family like?"

His shoulders shifted in a slight shrug. "Didn't have any brothers or sisters."

"But your parents? They're still alive?"

"Yes. Both my parents are attorneys. My father still practices and is on the board of directors of numerous businesses. My mother left her career when I was born but filled her spare time with various charities. They go to all the right parties and know all the right people."

"You don't get a along with them?"

"Actually, I love them a lot…we just don't have much in common. They wanted a different kind of life for me than I wanted for myself."

"Like what?"

"Ivy League schools, marrying well…having children who would carry on the family businesses and traditions."

"And what did you want?"

"I didn't know for a long time. I went to the schools they chose, dated the girls they approved of. Even got a degree in political science and was headed in the exact direction they wanted me to go."

"Did something happen to change your path?"

"Yes and no. I was a semester away from getting my master's degree and was set to start law school the next year. Then I met Harry."

"Who's Harry?"

"An Iraq war vet I met at one of my mother's charity events. He was a highly decorated soldier and sat at the table with us. He'd lost one leg and part of his arm in an IED blast. I remember thinking if that had happened to me, I'd think my life was over. But Harry was only a few years older than me and had already done remarkable things with his life. He was married, had a couple of kids, and instead of feeling sorry for himself, was working to make things better for returning soldiers. I, on the other hand, had come to the dinner because my mother made me. I was pissed because a couple of my friends had gone snow skiing and I wanted to go, too. And, oh yeah, my Porsche had a door ding. Those were my big problems."

"Sounds like Harry really made an impact on you."

"He did, much to my parents' and my fiancé's dismay."

Though she longed to ask about that fiancé, she wanted to hear more about Jake's life-changing decisions.

"What did you do?"

"I enlisted."

"Wow, that was gutsy."

"Not really. What I told you earlier was true. I didn't know what I was getting into. I only knew my life up to that point had been useless. I'd been breathing air and taking up space without any real contribution."

"How did your parents take the news?"

"They weren't happy but eventually accepted my decision."

"And your fiancé?"

"Broke it off with me."

"Seriously?"

"Yep. When it was clear I wasn't going to be providing her with the life she wanted, we both agreed it wasn't going to work."

"What a shallow woman she must have been."

Jake remembered Sarah's baby blue eyes swimming in tears as she pled with him to change his mind. She'd been a sweet girl who had expected a certain kind of life. He had no ill thoughts about her but he also knew his feelings for her hadn't been the long-lasting ones either. Their marriage never would have worked.

"She wasn't a bad person. She just wanted a different kind of life. But so did I."

"She obviously didn't love you."

That much was true. Their broken engagement had been a mere blip on his life, with barely any influence. Within six months of their break-up, Sarah was married to one of her father's junior law partners.

"How long were you in the Army?"

"Six years. I considered making a career of it but I came home on leave and—"

"And what?"

Jake shrugged. "I met someone and decided to do something else."

"Teresa?"

Jake released a slow breath. They were getting into territory he didn't want to go. He'd already shared more about his past than he ever had with any other person. Hell, even Teresa hadn't known about his terror before he'd been sent to Afghanistan or about the talk he'd had with the Army chaplain. He'd never considered the events something he would want to discuss. With Angela it had felt right. But there were certain areas he could not and would not talk about. Soon the discussion would be halted. He regretted that because he knew the sweet intimacy they were sharing would also end. However, going further into his past would only cause massive regret. He lived with his mistakes daily. Having them as a topic of conversation was out of the question.

Hoping to cut it off, his answer was abrupt. "We got married and I became a cop."

"What was your wife like?"

He closed his eyes and tried to picture Teresa's heart-shaped face. An ache started in his chest when he realized he couldn't. He could describe her but he couldn't see her in his mind. "She was very pretty, had a good sense of humor but was kind of quiet and on the shy side. She was a neonatal nurse. Loved her job." He shrugged. "We had some good times."

"You loved her very much."

"Yes."

"And then she died."

Jake loosened his arms but was unable to completely let her go. Being with Angela was a fantasy he never expected to come true. He'd certainly never planned to act on his desires but now that he had, damned if he wanted to end it, especially on a sour note.

Hoping he could cut off this line of questioning without ruining things, he said, "That's not a topic I want to talk about."

She was silent for so long, he wondered if he had hurt her feelings. Should have known Angela wouldn't back down.

"You feel responsible for her death."

He dropped his arms from her and rolled away. "Let it go, Angela."

"It wasn't your fault."

Jake went to his feet and pulled his pants on, refusing to answer. And, as usual, Angela persisted. "Her death was tragic but you're not to blame."

Whirling around, he glared down at the too beautiful, infinitely desirable, and extremely irritating woman on the bed. "What the hell do you know about it?"

Angela hurt for him. She wanted to call him back to bed and hold him until the pain went away. Even if she made the offer, from the look of fury on his face, he'd refuse the invitation. She debated evading his question or being vague about her knowledge. She couldn't do that. Though she had only this night learned she was a coward in certain situations, she refused to back away from this confrontation. Not facing the truth never accomplished anything.

"I know everything, Jake. You were a cop, protecting a witness—Suzanna Long. She was due to testify against a very powerful man in Chicago. Unfortunately several people in the police department were on his payroll, including your captain. Your house was bombed and Teresa was critically injured. You were at the hospital with her as she fought for her life. While you were on leave, others took over the case. Your witness was shot and killed on her way to the courthouse. And your wife died three days later without regaining consciousness."

He stared at her as if she were some kind of foreign being. She hastily explained, "It wasn't out of curiosity. I'm LCR's main researcher. I create the files on all LCR employees. That means I—"

"I know what it means. I just—" He shook his head. "Hell, you must think I'm the stupidest person alive. Here I was thinking I had some semblance of privacy and you know every damn thing about me."

"Because of my job, Jake. For no other reason."

"Well tell me this, Miss Information Gatherer. Do you also know that Teresa was two months pregnant with our first child? Did you know I beat the hell out of two of the men responsible, almost killing them?"

She felt sick. "No, I didn't know that."

His smile bitter, he shrugged into his shirt. "Sometimes the most salacious parts get missed by even the best and nosiest researchers."

"That's not fair."

"Yeah, life's like that."

His long strides took him out of the room in seconds and then she heard the adjoining door to his apartment open and then slam shut.

Angela dropped her head back onto her pillow. Running after him to apologize would be useless. Silly of her to feel guilty for having done her job—though it was clear she'd missed a few pertinent details. No, she shouldn't feel guilty for knowing as much as she did. What she did regret was not telling him sooner. Maybe that would have made all the difference and this night would have ended with them still wrapped in each other's arms.

She glanced at the bedside clock, amazed it was only three in the morning. She felt as if she'd lived a lifetime in just a few short hours. First her humiliating and career-ending panic, then her trip to the emergency room, followed by the incredibly erotic shower with Jake and the even more deliciously erotic lovemaking. And now the blow-up that put an end to their short romance, possibly even their friendship.

Exhaustion crept over her and she closed her eyes. Sleep was impossible. She had destroyed her career as an LCR operative. Had she lost Jake, too?

# Chapter Fourteen

He was a prick and not proud of it. Jake knew he had no good excuse for the way he'd behaved. Angela had given him her beautiful body. Instead of feeling damn lucky, he'd berated her for knowing his shitty past. Of course she knew it. And if he'd been thinking with his head instead of his dick the last few months, he would've known that.

She'd had a hell of a day. A scare, the loss of a dream, and an injury to her hand. And he, being the selfish, horny bastard that he was, had taken advantage of her vulnerability. If McCall were here, he'd give the man permission to kick his ass. And he was quite sure his boss would be happy to oblige.

After storming out of her bedroom, Jake had spent the rest of last night alternately cursing his naivety and blaming Angela for not telling him sooner that she knew about his past. Why let the little fact that she had been doing her job get in the way of his hurt pride? A couple hours ago, he'd come to the humbling conclusion that he was an idiot. She had done nothing wrong. He should have realized that she had delved into his background. And instead of being hesitant to have a man who'd fucked up so badly watch her back, she'd given him her total trust. Another humbling realization.

Yesterday had been all about bad judgment. He'd taken Angela to bed. Yes, it had been incredible, and so damn satisfying his sated body hummed with satisfaction and demanded more of the same. He couldn't act on those wants though.

It'd been a dumbass thing to do. There was no future for them. He had no plans to ever get serious with another woman, much less make any kind of long-term commitment. Giving in to those kinds of emotions wasn't something he could allow ever again. Losing Teresa had damned near destroyed him. If he let himself fall for Angela…Hell no, he couldn't let himself go there.

And Angela would want more than some occasional hot sex. She would want a future and he couldn't offer her one. She deserved to have everything she wanted—he just couldn't be the one who gave it to her.

But what he had to give her before another moment passed was an apology.

He knocked on their connecting door. A day ago, he would have walked in uninvited. After his asinine behavior, he wasn't sure of his welcome. She had every right to be pissed.

Instead of calling out for him to enter, she opened the door. Shadows lurked beneath her eyes telling him of her exhaustion, yet he saw no animosity in her expression.

She stepped back and said, "Come in. I just made coffee."

"I—" Jake blew out an explosive sigh. "Hell, Angela, I'm sorry about the way I acted. You did nothing wrong."

The smile she gave him was breathtakingly beautiful and full of understanding. "I should have told you before. I just didn't know how."

"And I was an idiot for not knowing."

"I would never discuss anything I learn with anyone. After I compile my report, I hand it off to Noah. We don't talk about it either."

Jake nodded. Angela was the most scrupulously honest and open person he'd ever known. "I figured that. And I appreciate you believing in me enough not to turn down being my partner. Others might have figured I wasn't up to the task since I failed to protect both Suzanna and Teresa."

"Stop blaming yourself for the horrible acts of others. You did nothing wrong."

Jake kept silent. He had trusted the wrong people and would regret that decision for the rest of his life.

"Help yourself to coffee. I'm almost finished packing."

"I want you to reconsider your decision to quit."

Angela had known this was coming. She had actually expected to have this discussion last night. After telling her about his early days in the Army, she figured he'd relate that back to how she had handled herself and try to explain away her ridiculous overreaction. Unfortunately, in the light of day, she still saw no correlation. At crunch time, he had come through for his country. She, on the other hand, had behaved like an untrained neophyte.

She shook her head. "I know what you're going to say, so save it. My panic attack over something as simple as a kid on a skateboard showed me who I am. If the killer came after me, I'd probably get myself killed and possibly someone else, too. I can't trust myself. You shouldn't trust me either."

"Hell, Angela, if you think LCR operatives operate without fear, you need to reevaluate your opinion of us. We might not go around talking about it, but I'd bet my last dollar there's not one of us who hasn't been scared at some point."

"But that doesn't stop you from doing your job. I was a basket-case, Jake. There's no other word for it. If that had been a real attack, I would have failed miserably."

Before he could object, she raised her hand and added, "Don't try to talk me out of it. I know my worth as an LCR employee. It's a role I'm comfortable with and excel at. That will be enough."

"Will it?"

She turned away from the penetrating look in his eyes. One would think they'd be awkward with each other since only hours ago they'd been as intimate as two people could be. Instead those delicious hours last night felt as far away as if they'd been another one of her fantasies. Even though her fantasies had never been so fulfilling or wonderful.

Making herself face him again, she said adamantly, "There's nothing else to do but go home. "

For several seconds, he maintained a hard, piercing stare. Finally he nodded. "Since we all traveled together on LCR's plane, I'll need to make commercial travel plans."

"Okay."

"But I'm going to make them for tomorrow."

"What?"

"You've had no downtime since we arrived. You're running on fumes. Let's take the day and enjoy London. We'll go home tomorrow."

The enticement of being with Jake for one more day was too irresistible to deny. His apology had been a surprise, but he'd given no indication their night of passion was something he wanted to repeat. Despite the feeling that she was delaying inevitable heartache, she couldn't help but say, "That sounds wonderful."

"Good. Get dressed and we'll be tourists for the day."

She felt his eyes on her until she disappeared into the bedroom. What would he do if she invited him back to bed for just a few hours? Could their connection be reestablished or was it gone for good? He had to be disappointed in her...she sure as hell was.

It was one of the best days of her life. Angela couldn't remember the last time she'd had such an easygoing, fun-filled day. After Jake booked the train tickets to Paris for the next afternoon, he'd returned to her apartment. She had been dressed and ready for him, eager to put her heartache behind her, at least for a little while.

As if determined to help her accomplish that goal, he set out on a quest for them to see as many sights as possible. Buckingham Palace, Big Ben, and Westminster Abbey were some of the ones she'd read about and had always longed to see. They were even more spectacular than what she had imagined.

In the early afternoon, they stopped at a pub for lunch and talked like two people who'd known each other forever. Once again, Jake didn't talk personal stuff and Angela didn't push. Easygoing was the word of the day and asking for more than he could give was a surefire way to spoil their fun.

After lunch, they walked down Dover Street and window-shopped, trying to outdo each other in finding the most outlandish and expensive items. Following a sign for a toy store down a side street, Angela found the perfect gift for Micah

McCall's birthday displayed in the window—an electric train set. She had been in his playroom many times and knew he didn't have one. He was going to love it.

As if it were the most natural thing in the world, she grabbed Jake's hand and dragged him into the store. Not that he looked the least bit unwilling…his eyes were as bright as a child's.

Once inside, they split up. Angela headed to examine the train and Jake couldn't take his eyes off a toy helicopter. She had a feeling they'd both be making a purchase today.

It didn't take long to determine that the train set was indeed the perfect gift for Micah. Before she made the purchase, she caught sight of a dollhouse that would put a big smile on Evie McCall's sweet little face.

Taking out her wallet, she handed the clerk her credit card. "I'd like to have these shipped to my home in Paris."

The clerk took down her information, promising delivery within the next week. Pleased with her purchases, Angela turned just in time to see Jake buying two helicopters. "Two?" she asked.

Looking younger than she'd ever seen him, he winked mischievously. "Feel like a little friendly competition in the park?"

Delighted at the idea, she accepted the challenge. "You're on."

They left the toy store the same way they'd entered, like two carefree children eager to continue their fun, never knowing that a killer watched and waited, just as eager for his chance to destroy.

# Chapter Fifteen

*Four days later*
*LCR Headquarters*
*Paris*

In thirty-six years of living, Noah had made his share of mistakes. Most times he took his knocks, cursing and growling the whole time. Being married to Samara had helped temper his responses. She teased him that he was mellowing but he preferred to think he'd grown wiser.

But even Mara couldn't help him put a better spin on this mistake. Neither of them had seen it coming. He wanted to hit something or someone—mostly himself. He shouldn't have put Angela on this op. For a new LCR operative, handling a serial killer case would be daunting. Coupled with the grief she was still experiencing, it was no wonder this had been a major bust. He had allowed her enthusiasm to override his usual caution. And now she was paying the price for his screw-up.

He had given her a few days off to think it over before she came in to see him, hoping the downtime would give her the distance she needed. Angela had a tendency toward impulsiveness. If she had simply made a rash decision about quitting, he wanted to give her plenty of time to reconsider. From the look on her face as she sat across from him, her decision was neither impulsive nor ill-considered. She no longer wanted to be an operative.

"Stop looking like that, Noah. You did nothing wrong."

"Hell yeah, I did something wrong. I shouldn't have put you on the op. You weren't ready."

"You don't understand. I'll never be ready. I proved that. At the first whiff of danger, I panicked."

"You just need more training to deal with that. I've seen plenty of operatives overreact."

She raised a questioning brow. "In the middle of a job?"

"No, and that's the issue. You need to learn how to stay in control at all times. Fright is a natural occurrence when one is threatened. You can learn to control your response. I can—"

She shook her head. "No, I appreciate the words but if it's all the same with you, I'd like to go back to my old job. That is, if you still want to keep me as an employee."

"Dammit, stop talking like that. Of course I want you as an employee. I'm just infuriated that you've lost your confidence."

Her mouth curved with her same jaunty smile but solemn sadness remained in her eyes. "I'm still as cocky and confident as ever. The only difference is I know what I can and can't do. It was a good lesson learned. I'm just sorry the bastard is still out there and I did nothing but hinder the case."

"You haven't hindered anything."

"How about everyone else? Any news from Eden, Shea, Sabrina or Riley?"

"No bites so far but we're not even two weeks into the mission. Fishing expeditions like these usually take a lot longer."

"I just hope something happens before he can take another victim."

"Jake didn't tell you? There's another woman missing."

"No, I guess he figured since I was out of the op, I didn't need to know."

"She's different from the others, in looks and profession. But she's been missing for several days and a dozen red roses were found in her apartment."

"Do they think he's changing his preferences?"

"Or expanding them. Hard to say until we know more."

"Or until he takes another one."

Noah shrugged. "That too."

"I wish I could have helped."

"We'll find him." Switching gears, he asked, "How did things go with Jake? You two get along okay?"

The flicker in her eyes gave him the answer. Something had happened between them. Question was, did it have anything to do with Angela's decision? Getting involved in his employees' personal lives wasn't the norm for him. Yeah, he'd been guilty of pairing operatives when he saw a unique chemistry between them but not since his debacle with Eden and Jordan years ago had he interfered with a relationship. However, if Angela's decision had been impacted because of her feelings for Jake, then he wanted to know.

"Jake's a great operative. I was lucky to have him as a partner for my one and only mission."

"Yet I can't help but think you might've made a different decision if I had partnered you with someone else."

"Absolutely not, Noah. My decision had nothing to do with my partner. If anything, Jake did his best to talk me out of quitting."

That was good to hear but until he talked with Mallory, he wouldn't be satisfied.

Angela carefully watched Noah's expression. Reading him was usually impossible but she had no trouble seeing what he was trying to do. He was looking for an out for her--a way to turn her failure around. Blaming himself or maybe even Jake instead of accepting that the mistake was all Angela's. It was all on her.

Jake would have to give a full report of their ruined mission. She didn't expect any special favors from him when he described her meltdown. Once Noah heard the detailed account, she was sure Noah would agree that she wasn't operative material, no matter how much she wished it otherwise.

On their last day in London, Jake had been nothing but kind. She had half expected him to try to talk her out of her decision again but he hadn't even mentioned LCR. Instead they'd played all day like two people who had nothing more on their minds but enjoying themselves. It had been exactly what she needed. Her only disappointment came at the end of the day when he'd kissed her forehead and told her what time to be ready to leave the next day. The train ride home had been equally uneventful. She'd caught a taxi from the train station and hadn't seen him since.

"Samara will be happy that you made it back safely. I'd like for you to visit with her."

Angela hid a grimace. Talking to Samara was something she usually welcomed. However, despite Noah's assurance that she had nothing to be ashamed of, Angela knew she was a huge disappointment to everyone at LCR. Admitting that to herself was hard enough. Discussing it with another person, especially someone whose respect meant so much, was entirely different. Yet she understood Noah's request.

She stood. "I'll make an appointment with her. And I want to thank you for your understanding, Noah. I'll do my best not to disappoint you ever again."

"Stop it, Angela. You didn't disappoint me this time. I just want to make sure you made the right decision for the right reasons."

A lump developed in her throat for this man who'd been her champion from the moment she met him. He might be her boss, but she had always felt as close to him as she would a big brother. No matter what he said, she knew she had let him down. And maybe that was what hurt most of all.

"Did you sleep with Angela?"

Jake had known McCall would want to talk about the failed op, but he never expected it to take such a personal tone. He shot up from his chair and glared at his boss. "Whether I slept with Angela or not is none of your damned business."

McCall barely raised a brow at Jake's explosion. "It is when it affects a mission."

Telling McCall that Angela had decided to quit before they slept together wasn't something he intended to do. What had happened between them was no one's business but their own.

"Angela's decision to quit was based solely upon her reaction to the skateboarder. I was as stunned by her decision as anyone. She'd given no indication that she was having second thoughts. She was professional at all times and I couldn't have asked for a better partner."

"I'm glad to hear that. I'd like to see her go back into the field when she's ready."

Dropping back into his chair, Jake shook his head. "She seemed certain that she would never be ready."

"Maybe."

"Anything new on the case?"

"Zero. If he were keeping up with his timeline, he should have taken another woman by now and Clarissa Eaton's body should have already been discovered. Then again, if he were acting in his normal way, Clarissa never would have been taken in the first place since she's nothing like his usual victim."

"Could be he's added a new type to his preferences."

"If that's the case, then he's going to be even more elusive. This woman is like thousands of women in the workforce."

"Want me back on the op with someone else?"

McCall shook his head. "No. Riley, Eden, Shea and Sabrina will stay on the case until he's caught. Be back here tomorrow morning at ten. There's a case in the States I'm considering. I should know more by morning. I was going to send Dylan but I know he'd rather stay in Paris with Jamie. Their baby is due next month."

That was another thing Jake liked about LCR. Their missions might be top secret and dangerous as hell but many of the operatives had families. Having someone to come home to after a grueling op could make all the difference in the mental health of an operative. That wasn't something he'd given a lot of thought to. Having been on his own for several years, not having someone to come home to was the norm for him. When he'd been a cop, coming home to Teresa hadn't been that great. She had worked as many or more hours than he had. He didn't even let himself think what it would feel like to have someone waiting on him. It was never going to happen, so what was the point?

Could that be one of the reasons for Angela's difficulty? Having no family to come back to made her more uncertain, less confident? No, that couldn't be it. She had said more than once that LCR was her family, so why—

A light bulb clicked on in his mind. Hell, it was no wonder Angela had failed at her first op. Last Chance Rescue *was* her family. And she would hold herself up to the standard of every LCR operative. That was a damn tough thing to live up to. The first time she had experienced a scare and panicked, she had probably thought of women like Eden St. Claire or Shea Bishop, two seasoned operatives. They would have handled the situation differently now but how would they have reacted if it was their first time out?

Jake went to his feet. "I'll see you tomorrow."

McCall's dark eyes narrowed. "I can't stop you from seeing Angela outside of work but you damn well better not break her heart."

How the hell the man knew he was going to see Angela wasn't something Jake even contemplated. The LCR leader sometimes read people like a damn psychic. However, his reasons for going to see Angela had nothing to do with romance and everything to do with her job.

He repeated what he'd told himself a million times before. "I'd die before I hurt Angela."

"And I'd be glad to assist you in getting there if you did."

Jake couldn't help but grin. As death threats went, it was one of the mildest ones he'd ever received. Mild though it was, he knew McCall spoke the truth. And if he hurt Angela, Jake figured he deserved it.

She was being followed.

Angela picked up the pear from the trunk of her car that had fallen from her grocery bag. Pretending to examine the fruit for bruises, she peeked out of the corner of her eye. Yes, there he was. A man, maybe six feet tall, with shaggy, light brown hair, wire-rimmed glasses and a goatee. He was in a parking space a few yards away, looking under the hood of a white Volkswagen van. He seemed immersed in his tasks, however, as she turned her head away, she saw his gaze zero in on her again.

This was the third time she had seen him. The first time was two days ago when she'd been window-shopping on Rue Beaurepaire. She had spotted him standing at a doorway across the street from her. She had paid little attention. Years of men staring at her had accustomed her to their curious or glazed expressions. Having long legs and exotic features seemed to attract a certain kind of gawker and she'd had her share over the years. With so much on her mind, she had dismissed him as just another leerer. But she recalled a man of medium height and build, fair-skinned, and wispy, light brown hair.

Yesterday, she had run errands and had seen a man standing across the street from her dry cleaners. Since there was no bus stop or even a business close by, she had briefly wondered why he stood there. Then her cellphone had rang, distracting her. She'd grabbed it from her purse and when she'd looked up, he was gone.

She remembered that he had been dressed as a heavy-set tourist. A camera and binoculars hung from his neck, and he had a head full of thick, curly blond hair. Today he was more slender, slightly taller, had a receding hairline and wore glasses. Admittedly the three descriptions didn't sound remotely similar. Make-up, wigs, facial hair, extra padding and shoe lifts were easily accessible items and could make a person look completely different.

Her operative training had included not only learning to disguise her appearance but also recognizing identity concealment in others. Too bad that training hadn't kicked in earlier. Angela knew in her gut that she was looking at the same man from the two other occurrences. And this time, he had followed her home.

The Red Rose Killer? No, of course not. How could that be? She had received no roses. Besides, why would he have followed her from London? How could he have gotten her address? No one, not even Roddy, Club Drago's manager, knew where she lived.

This didn't make sense at all. She told herself she was being paranoid. That she was seeing a killer in some innocuous stranger. Her brain said it just wasn't possible. Her intuition told her something else.

The same man, in three different disguises, within the course of three days? Who else could it be but the killer? Despite all the odds and her massive screw-up, she had actually managed to attract him. And he had come all the way to Paris for her. She had studied everything there was to know about this man. This behavior was completely out of the norm for him. Noah had told her a woman unlike his usual victim had been abducted. That could mean a lot of things but it could also mean that he was changing or expanding his preferences and routine.

Not for a second did she question whether she should play this out. She had no choice. She would do what she had been trained to do. Shoving aside all the doubts and fears she'd heaped on herself the last few days, she slipped a hand in her coat pocket, located her cellphone, and pressed Jake's speed-dial number. Then, taking the wireless earbud she had attached to the phone, she acted as if she were pushing her hair behind her ear and clipped it on.

Jake answered on the first ring. "Hey, I'm glad you called. I'm headed your way. I need to talk—"

She kept her voice low and calm. "He's here."

"Where?" he asked sharply.

She appreciated Jake's quick comprehension. "The parking lot of my apartment complex."

"How close is he?"

"About thirty yards away."

"Does he know you've seen him?"

"I don't think so. He's pretending to work on his van. This is the third time I've seen him. The first time, I was window-shopping and I thought he was just some creep leering at me. Then yesterday, at the dry cleaners, this man was staring at me from across the street. Again I dismissed him. Both times, he was disguised, but I'm sure it was the same man. And now, here he is again."

Would Jake believe her or had he lost all confidence in her?

"Shit. Shit. Shit."

"What's wrong?"

"I'm halfway across town. It'll take me at least ten minutes to get to you. I'm texting McCall to see if he can get someone to you sooner."

Even as he said the words, Angela knew there wouldn't be enough time. If she continued to loiter in the garage, he would become suspicious and possibly leave. She couldn't risk that happening. She was going to have to do this on her own.

"I can do this, Jake."

"You have your weapon?"

"Yes, of course."

"Okay. Wait till he comes at you. Then hold your gun on him until I—"

"What? No, Jake, he still has a victim. We have to go with our original plan."

"We sure as hell do not," Jake snapped. "We'll bring the bastard in and get him to talk."

"And if he won't, what then? If there's a chance to rescue this woman, we need to take it."

"He wouldn't have brought her all the way to Paris. *Think, Angela!* He's probably already dumped her body somewhere. The most important thing is to capture the bastard before he can kill anyone else."

"If this was another LCR operative, would you say the same thing?"

The briefest of pauses gave her the answer.

"I'm going to let him take me. You can track me. He's acting so against type, there's a possibility he could have the woman with him."

"Absolutely not. I can't allow—"

"Look, I know you have no reason to believe me, but I need you to trust me, Jake. I can do this."

"Angela, I said, no. That's an order."

"This might be our only chance." When he didn't answer, she added softly, firmly, "Jake, please…I can do this. I know I can."

Instead of arguing, he said grimly, "Describe him."

"A little over six feet tall, but he's wearing lifts because yesterday he was a couple of inches shorter. He's wearing a badly cut brown wig with a receding hairline, fake goatee, and wire-rimmed glasses. Yesterday he wore padding, had a bulbous nose and thick, curly hair; today he's much thinner and has a beaky nose, which looks to be his own. And the first time I saw him, he was medium build and height with brown, thinning hair."

Even though it sounded as though she were describing three different people, she was relieved when Jake's only comment was "That's probably how he's stayed hidden for so long. Sounds like he's damn good with disguises."

"He's in an older white Volkswagen van, maybe about five years old."

"Can you see a license plate?"

"No, not from here."

"Anything else stand out?"

"Looks like there's a small dent on the left rear bumper." She stretched her neck ever so slightly…it was awfully hard to look without appearing as if she were looking. "That's all I can see."

"Is there anyone else in the garage with you?"

"No. And I can't stall any longer."

"I don't want—"

"Jake, please. I know I haven't given you any reason to trust me, but I promise you, I can do this."

Silence filled her ear for several taut seconds and then he said, "You have your trackers?"

Relieved, she answered, "My necklace and watch. My phone too but he'll probably dispose of it." And because, despite his obvious misgivings, he was going to approve her plan, she whispered, "Thank you."

Another long tense silence and then his ragged sigh exploded in her ear. "Partners don't thank each other until the op is over. Got it?"

Withdrawing the grocery bag from her car, Angela knew she had dawdled as long as she dared. She might be on her own but she would never be alone. At that thought a surge of warmth and comfort surrounded her. LCR was the best in the business and she trusted Jake with her life. Not for a moment would this be a solo mission.

Jake gripped the phone in his hand as he stared at the scene in front of him. Miles of stalled traffic and he was caught in the middle lane, in between two semi-trucks. No way in hell could he get to her in time.

"Dammit, now I'm stuck in a traffic jam."

"Just track me as soon as you can. I'll be fine. Really."

Wanting to scream his frustrations, he forced himself to focus on making sure she knew her options. "Don't let it go too far. If it's between your survival and his, don't hesitate. Take him down. Kill him if you have to. Understand?"

"Yes."

He had thought watching Angela dance and strip in front of a roomful of salacious strangers was torturous. That was nothing compared to listening as a killer stalked her and being unable to do a damn thing about it.

McCall and three LCR operatives were headed to her apartment but they were even further away than Jake. No one would reach her in time. This man would act way before anyone could get to her. Would the bastard follow Angela up to her apartment and play out the same scenario as he had with the other victims? If so, what had he done with Clarissa Eaton? There was no damn way he would have brought her all the way to Paris. Would her body be discovered soon since he was about to abduct a new victim?

When this was over, he'd kick his own ass for not considering that the killer had already targeted Angela. Had he been stalking her the entire time they were in London? How the hell had the man known her address in Paris? Could he have been on the train with them? Why had he not given any consideration that the bastard would come after her? Just because the maniac was acting against type meant nothing. Dammit, he should have stayed with Angela until the creep had been caught. If this went to shit, it was all on him.

Jake breathed out a ragged breath. Dissection of his piss-poor handling of the situation would have to wait for another day. The most important thing right now was making sure Angela stayed alive.

This was as far from their carefully controlled scenario as it could be. He had planned to be with her every step of the way. And despite his anger at her for disobeying him, he would back her up. When this was over, they'd damn well have a discussion about her following orders. For now, he had to trust that she could handle this. He had no other choice.

"Okay," she said softly. "I'm headed up to my apartment. Stairs or elevator?"

"Stairs. I don't want you on the elevator with him."

"Okay."

"Go silent. No talking to me after this."

"K." She paused a beat and then added, "See you soon."

Hell, he hoped so. Horns blared as impatient drivers let their displeasure be heard. Jake's total focus was on the sounds coming from his cellphone. Angela's breathing, a door opened, then closed. Footsteps, light ones and then, though distant, he heard the distinct clop of heavier feet. Then the most ominous sound of all—a man's voice.

Never had Jake felt more helpless than to listen as the woman he'd come to care about more than he'd ever thought possible was attacked by a serial killer.

# Chapter Sixteen

As he followed the tall, beautiful Angela to her apartment, he smiled to himself. Everything was working perfectly now. How could he have doubted his Dark Angel?

Three days ago, roses in hand, he had arrived at her apartment building in London, ready to begin their courtship. What he observed was his Dark Angel leaving with one of the mammoth men who had rescued her from the over-amorous drunk at Club Drago. The same man he had seen her shopping with the day before. Their car was packed with luggage. He had followed them to the train station and watched, devastated, as she and the man boarded a train for Paris. Only by sheer will had he not returned to his home and destroyed everything.

Fortunately, good reason had prevailed. He had returned to the toy store where she had purchased an electric train set and dollhouse the day before. He'd been preoccupied, so careful to hide in the shadows from her behemoth male companion, that he had paid little note when she'd asked that the gifts be delivered to Paris.

It had taken little effort to obtain her name and address. After subduing the store clerk and tying him up, in minutes he had accessed the paid accounts. His Dark Angel's name was Angela Delvecchio. Then came the realization of her gift to him. Because of their phenomenal connection, she was already making his life easier without his even asking. She had known he needed to leave London and was simply leading him to a new home.

The most time-consuming aspect had been making a major move in such a short amount of time. Used to traveling with large quantities of wardrobe changes, hiding a young woman in a secret compartment was child's play. No one paid attention to an elderly man struggling with giant trunks other than offers of assistance. He loved that there were still polite people in the world. Courtesy often seemed to be a lost art.

Now he had the blonde woman with him and would soon introduce her to his new companion. He didn't question why he had to take his Dark Angel now, at this very moment. It was a compulsion and he'd learned over the years never to deny his needs. When he was younger, he had warred with himself over satisfying his desires. He had been content because he'd had all he needed. Then when he had lost everything, the door to those long-suppressed desires became unchained. The needs that had been simmering for years were unfettered, set free from their bonds. This was his calling. Since coming to that realization, he had taken what he wanted and was a happier man for it.

The reward for his hard work was almost at hand. He had found a place in Reims, about four hours outside Paris. The mansion was old but well preserved, the atmosphere perfect for his needs. Everything was coming together as if destiny had taken over.

And now for the plat de résistance.

He approached her quietly. "Pardon moi," he said meekly, friendly.

His Dark Angel turned; eyes the color of decadent, dark chocolate widened with surprise. Oh yes…she was even more exquisite up close. Any remaining doubts that this was 'the one' disappeared.

Holding her hand to her chest, she gasped. "Oh, you startled me. I had no idea anyone was around."

He was pleased that she spoke English. His knowledge of French was modest at best. Not being able to communicate his needs would have hindered their relationship. And her voice…it was even better than he could have anticipated. Rich, cultured, with a husky timbre. It would take almost no effort to train her.

His smile timid, he said, "I do apologize. I just moved in two doors down and can't get my phone to work. Do you have a cellphone I could use to call the telephone company?"

"Of course." Her head bent, she rummaged around in her purse. "I know it's here somewhere."

She was wearing the perfect apparel for what he needed. Her jacket, though modest, covered a beautiful low-necked blouse and gave him access to the smooth, creamy area between her neck and shoulder. He struck swiftly, jabbing the hypodermic needle deep into the muscle.

She yelped and jumped back. "What did you…?" In seconds, her eyes glazed and she stumbled backward, away from him.

He reached for her, expecting a brief, futile struggle as the drug took hold. Designed to disorient but not cause unconsciousness, his Dark Angel would be pliable and open to his suggestions within a couple of minutes. To his dismay she put up no struggle at all. Her arms went limp and her purse and grocery bag fell to the floor.

In the voice many had called beautiful and mesmerizing, he commanded, "Come with me," and held out his hand. Once more, his Dark Angel proved that she was meant to be with him as, like magic, she took his hand and allowed him to lead her down the hallway and to the stairwell.

Anyone who saw them would believe they were a couple in love, going out for a stroll. Someday that's how it would be. Someday very soon, she would no longer need the drugs. She would be his and he would be hers.

Opening the back of the van, he helped her inside and then uncovered the flooring where the blonde woman lay in her trunk. He felt his Dark Angel stiffen. "Don't worry, my love. This is just a temporary home for you."

He pushed her to her knees. She went willingly, just as he knew she would. Since the hiding space was small, he quickly removed her jacket along with any superfluous apparel. Shoving her forward, she fell on top of the blonde woman, who screeched at the intrusion. The sounds muffled by the tape covering her mouth.

He replaced the lid and then the flooring, covering the two very different looking but equally important women. One would be the culmination of his recent work and the other would be his salvation.

With every ounce of her strength, Angela fought to cling to reality while whatever drug he had injected her with worked just as hard to distort her thinking. As soon as he'd plunged the needle into her, she had begun reciting three things in her mind, repeatedly: *My name is Angela Delvecchio. I work for Last Chance Rescue. LCR is tracking me—I am not alone.*

If she had any chance of success, maintaining hold of this information was imperative.

Though what she wanted most to do was just drift in this euphoric wonderland the drug had created, she forced her mind to focus on tangibles. Someone was beneath her, wiggling. The compartment was filled with an impenetrable darkness and almost no additional space to move, but she managed to shift slightly, giving the woman beneath her an opportunity to breath. Smothering the victim she was supposed to rescue was probably against LCR regulations.

Rescue? Yes, she was here on a rescue mission. She had been drugged and the woman beneath her had been abducted. It was up to Angela and Jake to save her.

*Jake.* She focused on him, pictured his face, imagined his voice. Remembered his wonderful strength. He was her partner, her friend…her lover. She was not alone.

The body beneath her made muffled noises and it took several seconds of wondering before Angela figured out that the woman's mouth was covered with something. Lifting a lethargic, uncooperative arm, Angela raised her hand to where the noise was located and felt something—tape. Tugging and pulling, she managed to uncover half of her mouth.

Of all the things she expected the woman to say, it wasn't, "Oh please, get your knee out of my stomach."

"Sorry," Angela mumbled.

Focusing with all her might, she told her leg to shift and figured she had been successful when the woman blew out a relieved sigh, which turned into a rush of words. "My name is Clarissa Eaton. Who are you? Why has he taken us? What's he going to do? Who is he? Why did—"

"Hold on." Angela swallowed. The drug clawed at her mind, pulling her deeper and deeper into a sluggish daze. Her tongue thick and dry, she swallowed again and said slowly, thickly, "My name is Angela. I work for..." Ah, dammit, who did she work for? Squeezing her eyes tight, she said, "I work for a company... we'll help you."

"A company? What do you mean?"

Shit. She had to get her focus back. Biting her lip till she tasted blood, the pain jerked her into reality once more. "My name is Angela Delvecchio. I work for Last Chance Rescue. We're not alone."

There, she'd said it. For some reason, the woman stayed frozen. Why wasn't she reassured by her declaration?

Angela tried again. "Jake, my lover." She shook her head. "I mean my partner... is tracking us."

"I don't understand. Why is your lover tracking you?"

With all of her faculties in tact, explaining her complicated relationship with Jake would be difficult. Drugged and jammed into a compartment barely large enough for one person, much less two, Angela knew a lucid, succinct response was impossible. She settled for "Forget the other stuff. Bottom-line, help is on the way."

"Who is this man that's taken us? Do you know?"

"Don't know his name. He's been killing women in London."

"What?" Clarissa screeched.

"Shh. Keep your voice down." Being blunt was probably a side effect of the drug. Any other time, Angela was almost sure she would have broken the news that they had been abducted by a serial killer in a more tactful way.

Soft sobs of despair came from Clarissa.

Grinding her teeth together to keep from falling into a drugged abyss, Angela said carefully, slowly, "We will escape. Promise. Keep calm. K?"

"Yes…all right."

"Can you tell me where you've been…what's happened since he took you?"

"Some things are hazy. I remember a policeman came to my house and told me an emergency call had come from my residence. I had my television up too loud and I went to turn it off so I could explain that the call hadn't come from me. I turned around and there he was, behind me. I don't remember much after that…he must have drugged me.

"When I came to, I was lying on some kind of table. He removed my clothes. He kept saying the reason he took me would soon be revealed. Since then, I think he's transported me to various places. I remember the sound of an engine and the feeling of movement beneath me."

"What about water…food? Has he allowed you either?"

"A little water, almost no food. He's taken me to the bathroom twice a day and holds me while I go."

She whispered the last sentence as though embarrassed.

"His shame…not yours."

"What are we going to do?"

"My hands and legs are free. He lets us out…I'll take care of him. Stay out of the way."

"All right," Clarissa whispered. "Thank you."

Angela spoke with more confidence than she felt. Whatever the maniac had given her continued to play havoc with her thinking. And just from the small movements she'd managed to make inside the compartment, she doubted that her limbs would be cooperative when he released them from the box. Yet she had no choice, Clarissa was counting on her.

Without warning, the drug slammed through her with the force of an avalanche and she plunged into another world. Reality ceased to exist. Time stopped. Dramatic but realistic hallucinations took control as one by one, her entire family came for a visit. They sat down and chatted with her. Simple, innocuous conversations but so unbelievably, wonderfully real.

A continuous, softly spoken voice in her head told her it wasn't real but she pushed it aside as she drifted in a euphoric, comforting haze, chatting with the loved ones she missed so much.

Minutes or hours later, she opened her eyes to see her mother across from her again. A small part of her mind whispered that the conversation wasn't possible, but it felt so wonderful and natural, she went with the delusion.

No, no. She had to stop. Something was wrong. Gathering up enough comprehension to remember she was in trouble, she asked, "What should I do, Mama?"

Her mother gave a gentle, teasing smile and opened her mouth. Angela tensed, ready for whatever assistance her mother could offer. What followed was a recitation of an old family recipe for corn chowder.

Not exactly helpful information when trying to escape from a serial killer.

Jake stood at the door of Angela's apartment and stared down at the evidence of her abduction. A bag of groceries lay spilled on the floor. Her purse, cellphone and earbud were scattered around, close to the bag. McCall should be here any minute with additional operatives. As soon as they arrived, the trace would begin.

Only a couple of minutes after hearing Angela's abduction, Jake had been able to maneuver his way around the semi-trucks and get off on the shoulder of the road. Driving like a madman, he had broken a half dozen traffic laws in the vain hope that he could reach Angela's apartment complex before she disappeared with her abductor. The whole time he had known it was too late but he'd prayed for all he was worth that he was wrong. Unfortunately he had been right.

Did the bastard plan to travel back to London with her? Had he already disposed of Clarissa Eaton's body? If so, Angela's abduction would be for nothing.

He shoved his fingers through his hair. What the hell was he going to do if something happened to her? He shouldn't have agreed to let her carry out the op. He should have demanded she take the monster down. What if he never saw her alive again? Was he, once again, going to be responsible for getting someone he cared about killed? Hell, did he have some kind of black cloud hanging over his head?

Jake jerked himself out of the useless blame game. Having played that game hundreds of times before, he knew it accomplished nothing. He needed to focus on the positives. Angela was stronger than she gave herself credit for. She could take this bastard out if need be. And they were going to trace her whereabouts. They would find her and everything would be okay. He had to believe that.

The cellphone in his hand rang and in an instant, Jake answered, "Mallory."

"I'm three minutes from her flat," McCall said. "Meet me out front."

He grabbed Angela's belongings and turned away. Running down the hallway, he was in the lobby and on the sidewalk in less than a minute. A black SUV pulled to the curb and McCall got out. "You drive…I'll track her."

Sliding in behind the steering wheel, Jake took off the second the other man got into the passenger side.

"Head to the A4," McCall said. "She's about twenty minutes ahead of us."

As he weaved in and out of the heavy evening traffic, Jake did his best not to think about what Angela was going through. If he allowed himself to go down that path, he wouldn't be able to function. She was counting on him and he'd damn well not let her down.

Grim and silent, McCall sat beside him and stared at the laptop screen. Three other operatives followed in another SUV. Between the five of them, no way was this bastard going to get away.

Was she drugged and unconscious or awake and aware? Having seen her fear up close and personal, he could only imagine how terrified she must be.

Dammit, he should have seen this coming. Just because they had quit the op didn't mean the killer had.

Without looking up from the screen, McCall said gruffly, "Stop beating yourself up. The man's acting completely against type. No one could have predicted he would follow her to Paris. How the hell did he even know her address?"

Jake's mind searched for the oddity and then closed his eyes briefly. "The presents."

"What presents?"

"The day before we returned to Paris, Angela and I went shopping. She found gifts for your kids and asked for them to be shipped to her apartment in Paris. He must've been in the store and overheard."

"Shit," McCall said softly.

Bile surged up his throat. Instead of watching for the killer, he'd been concentrating on Angela, wanting to make her feel better…see her laugh again. And now he didn't know if he'd ever see her alive again. "Dammit, I should have been watching her back."

"Before we were married, Mara was taken right before my eyes. I was there to protect her and ended up almost getting her killed."

The expression on the man's face kept Jake from asking for details. Whatever had happened, it still haunted him.

"Thing is, no matter how prepared you think you are, shit happens. Angela has been trained to handle the unexpected, just like any operative."

"Hell, McCall, how can you say that after what happened in London?"

The LCR leader shrugged. "I've known her for years. Know what she's made of. She's strong. And she'll come through this even stronger."

Jake didn't respond. McCall hadn't seen Angela after her scare. There was no way she was anything but terrified. Just because she had assured him she could do this didn't mean it was true. He had to get to her before the maniac caused her even more damage. Determination settled in his gut…nothing would stop him from saving her.

McCall hissed a vicious curse.

"What?"

When McCall didn't answer, Jake shot him a look. The bleak expression in his eyes chilled Jake's blood.

"What the hell's wrong?" Jake barked.

"The GPS went dark. We have no way to track her."

The determination in Jake's gut turned to dust. Angela was on her own.

# Chapter Seventeen

The cessation of movement jolted Angela back to consciousness and reality. Like the first sprinkle of raindrops before a downpour, half-formed facts appeared in her mind. The Red Rose Killer. Abduction. Drugged.

She shook her head to clear it and full knowledge of the events poured down on her. How long had she been unconscious? When had the van stopped? Would he leave them here in this hellish box or let them out? She remembered that in one of her more lucid moments, she had tried to lift the top with her back. It hadn't budged. Until he deemed it time to let them out, they were here for the duration.

"Clarissa, are you awake?"

"Yes. Thank God you are, too. We've been traveling forever and you've been mumbling about all sorts of bizarre things."

"Sorry. Whatever he drugged me with made me hallucinate."

"Are you feeling better?"

"Yes."

"Will you be able to fight him when he lets us out?"

The hope in Clarissa's voice was painful to hear—all the more because Angela wasn't sure of the answer. Without drugs, she could handle the maniac, no problem. But she was still disoriented. On top of that, her extremities had gone numb. The moment she was released from this compartment, she'd love to think she could spring out of here and take the killer down. Truth was, she didn't know if her legs would hold her.

"I'm going to do my best."

"What..." Clarissa cleared her throat and asked, "What does he do to his victims?"

Facing reality was one thing, but Angela saw no point in describing the horrific things this monster had done to his other victims. Apparently Clarissa wasn't one to watch television news or read newspapers. What the women went through before their deaths had been all too accurately reported. What purpose would it serve for her to know that he tortured his victims in a variety of ways before he slit their throats?

"There's no need for you to worry about that. We're going to get out of here, I promise."

Silence descended. How long was he planning to keep them in this box? He couldn't travel all the way back to London, could he? If he tried, she'd scream bloody murder until someone heard them.

"How did he get you to Paris?"

Clarissa gasped softly. "We're in Paris?"

"Yes. At least, we were."

"I don't know. I've been so out of it."

The monster had kept this poor woman in a box for how long? "Has he let you out at all?"

"I know I've been to the bathroom and I've had something to drink. Not sure how or when."

A sound outside the compartment made both women stiffen with dread. Though unbearably uncomfortable, within the confines of the compartment they had felt relatively safe. Footsteps and other noises were dreadful reminders that this man had something evil planned for them.

As the top of the compartment rattled, indicating they were about to look upon the eyes of their abductor once more, Angela issued final instructions: "Stay out of the way and don't draw attention to yourself. If you get the chance to run, don't hesitate. Run like hell. Find a place to hide. Remember, help is on the way."

As the lid was lifted, Angela whispered one last instruction "Be brave" but wasn't sure if that was for Clarissa or for herself.

"Welcome to my world." Derrick Delacourte smiled down at the two women who would soon fulfill his dreams. His Dark Angel lay on her stomach and he couldn't see her face. The blonde woman looked up at him with equal parts awe and dread. Soon it would be total awe as she came to know him better.

Grabbing his Dark Angel's shoulders, he pulled her up and dragged her from the van. She was limp, still dazed from the drug. He tried to stand her on her feet but her limbs were understandably numb from her confinement. Unfortunately, until he could get her restrained, he had no choice but to continue the drugs. One arm wrapped securely around her, he reached for the hypodermic needle lying on the table beside him. Just a bit more until he had everything in place.

Agony erupted in his head. Stunned, his arms loosened. What had happened? He couldn't get a grip on where the hurt had come from. Confused, he touched his face, then looked down at his hand. Why was there blood on his fingers?

Piercing pain shot through his leg. Horror filled him at the scissors sticking out of his thigh. Letting go a bellow filled with denial and betrayal, he jerked the scissors from his leg and lashed out with his fist, striking something hard.

The haze of rage cleared. Blinking rapidly, he looked down at the lump on the floor. His Dark Angel. *She* had done this to him?

Her legs were useless. Pins and needles shot through them with relentless stabs. The screaming curses above her indicated she had been able to do some damage to the bastard. Not enough though. The head-butt had disoriented him, giving her freedom. Unfortunately her legs hadn't held firm. On the way to the floor, her blurry eyes had spotted the scissors less than a foot away. She had lurched forward, managing to grab the handle and thrust it toward the nearest body part she could find.

Helplessly, she glared at her unmoving legs. Why wouldn't they budge? She shouted out loud to herself: "Get up, get up, get up!" Nothing moved. The little energy she'd had was gone. Only pain remained.

She tried to look up at him and could barely see...something was in her eyes. Touching her face, she realized she was bleeding. Then she remembered the pain in her head...he had hit her with something. When? That's why she couldn't think straight...why her limbs refused to work. She closed her eyes, uncertain if she would ever open them again. Clarissa would die because of her. Noah, Jake and the entire LCR organization would be disappointed in her forever.

*Jake?* Wait. Wasn't he coming? Yes, he was tracking her signal. He would be here soon. He wouldn't let her down. She told herself to hang on. Jake would rescue her. She wasn't alone.

With that reassurance, Angela closed her eyes, sure that when she woke again, she and Clarissa would be rescued and all would be well.

Consciousness returned and misery consumed her. She opened her bleary eyes. She was strapped to a table. Cold…she was so cold. Her teeth chattered as her body shuddered with chills. With every shudder, her head pounded. Dear heavens, her head was going to explode.

Lights blazed everywhere. Squinting, barely able to handle the glare, she looked around. Some kind of basement? A dank and musty smell hung in the air and an insidious coldness pervaded the entire room, as if the iciness was an entity all its own. Other than three large traveling trunks stacked against a wall and a few displaced bricks, the room was empty.

How long had she been unconscious? Where was the monster? Was Clarissa still alive?

Her mouth dry, her lips felt parched and cracked as though she'd been in the sun for hours. She swallowed, hoping for moisture and found none. Opening her mouth, she said hoarsely, "Clarissa?"

No answer.

Was she already dead? Where were Jake and Noah? Why hadn't they found them yet? She had been sure when she woke all of this would be over. Why did her head hurt so much?

"You're awake." The hard, cold voice sounded nothing like before. When he had taken her, his voice had been warm, eerily loving. Now, there was contempt and a seething fury.

"Where am I?"

"You have no right to ask questions. If you continue to talk, I'll close your mouth with tape. Do you understand?"

She nodded, wincing at the pain even that little amount of movement gave her.

"I'm deeply disappointed in you. You behaved terribly and must be punished. You've caused me great heartache. I've taken your clothes from you. I normally allow covering but your punishment prevents that. Once I'm through with you, I have no doubt you'll be much more amenable."

Her clothes? Pushing aside the nauseating ache in her head, she twisted her head and looked at her wrist. Her watch was gone. A growing horror spiraling through her, she glanced down at her chest. The silver medallion necklace should be lying between her breasts. It was gone, too.

She forced calmness. The jewelry was still here, with her clothes. He had probably just bundled them together and put them away somewhere. LCR could still track her. However, she had to be sure. "My watch and necklace, where are they?"

"Time is of no importance now that you're with me and your necklace was ugly and common."

"Where is my jewelry?" she demanded.

"I threw them out, along with your clothes. From now on, everything that touches your skin will come from me."

"When?"

"When what?"

The horror taking control within her once more, she spoke through clenched teeth, "When did you take my watch and necklace?"

"When I first took you, of course. I threw them, along with your coat, into a small river as we left Paris."

Why hadn't she noticed he'd taken them? That was why LCR hadn't come busting in to save them. They had no way to track her. She was at the mercy of this maniac without any back-up. Dear God, what was she going to do?

Pushing past the panic, she whispered, "Where's Clarissa?"

"She's in another room, sleeping. She's much more comfortable than you are."

"Where are we?"

"In my home."

"You live in France?"

"Of course not. I live in England."

"What does that mean? Where are we?"

"Silence!" he bellowed. "You will not question me further."

Before she could come up with perhaps an appeasing statement, he slapped duct tape over her mouth. She paid little attention to the indignity, as she got her first real look at the monster. He was no longer disguised and she recognized him. It was the policeman from London--the one who had helped her up when the skateboarder had knocked her down. Clarissa had said that a policeman had come to her home, with the ruse of an emergency call. Was this how he got into the women's homes? Disguising himself as a cop?

Angela watched a transformation take place as tears filled his eyes and his mouth contorted with sorrow. "You were supposed to be the one...the special one. You were going to launch us into stardom. Yet you've behaved horribly. Worse than any of the others." In an instant, the tears disappeared and an unholy evil gleamed in his brownish-green eyes turning them into a murky mud color. "However, if you survive the auditions, you might be able to come with me after all. The cleansing ritual has never failed me yet. We'll just have to wait and see."

Auditions? Cleansing ritual? That didn't sound like it involved soap and water. The thought of this evil creature touching her in any way sent shivers throughout her body and roiled her stomach. No way in hell would she allow him to do anything to her. He thought a bump on his nose and a scissor stab hurt? He would soon learn that he had abducted the wrong woman. When she was through with him, he wouldn't be able to steal a candy bar much less another human being.

Where this surge of courage came from she didn't know. How could she feel confident when she was tied so tightly and help wasn't coming? The answer came like a whisper. All of her LCR life, she had envisioned a time when it would just be her and evil and she would prevail. The breakdown in London with Jake had been an anomaly. She was Angela Delvecchio, LCR operative and one very kick-ass woman. This bastard would rue the day he selected the Dark Angel as his prey.

She heard a scratching sound and then the air was filled with the scent of lit matches.

He stood at the end of the table, holding a candle in his hand. "This is your first audition. Let's see how you fare."

Hot flames licked at her foot. Arching her entire body, she struggled against her bonds, the flesh at her wrist tearing as she tried to escape the searing pain. Then more heat, more flames... Agony shot through her. Every confident thought disintegrated. Closing her eyes, Angela screamed behind the tape: *Jake, where are you?*

# Chapter Eighteen

Jake had lost his mind long ago. The second Angela's GPS signal disappeared, he'd been in a free fall. Where the hell was she? And most important, was she still alive?

Since then, he'd been existing on adrenaline and not much more. The longer it took to find her, the more hopeless he felt.

Everyone in Europe was on the lookout. Border patrols for England, Germany, Italy and Spain swore no one matching the description of the van or its driver had come into their country. But who the hell knew if that was correct? The little information Jake had been able to provide was piss-poor and almost useless—a white van and a Caucasian male of indeterminate age who could disguise himself. Not exactly solid clues to identify and find a killer.

He and McCall were holed up in a hotel in Reims, France—the city they'd been headed when the GPS signal stopped. A sorry-assed location if the bastard had changed directions or managed to cross into another country. But it was all they could do until something came up.

And when they did find her, he was never letting her go. How damn arrogant and stupid he'd been. As if denying his feelings could make them any less real. He wanted to be with Angela, in every way possible. Period.

The hotel door swung open. Jake whirled around to face McCall. The man looked as haggard and worn as Jake felt.

"From the look on your face, the news isn't good," Jake said.

McCall had met with the special branch of detectives assigned to this case. His sigh of disgust was loud enough to be heard in the next room. "They have jack-shit, just like we do."

Jake returned his gaze to the computer screen. He felt as if he'd looked at the registration of every white van ever purchased or rented in Europe. Deidre had done the bulk of the research but all names that needed further investigation she'd forwarded to Jake.

Angela had described the vehicle as an older Volkswagen van, possibly five years old. Had the killer purchased the van when he arrived in Paris? Had he ferried over in it from England? Had he stolen the damn thing? Jake clicked profile after profile. Five LCR operatives were dedicated to checking any leads but so far there'd been too damn few.

Useless. This was all so fucking useless. There wasn't a person with that vehicle description that remotely matched the—

Another profile popped up on the screen. A middle-aged actor named Derrick Delacourte had rented a Volkswagen van in Paris five days ago. Delacourte had enjoyed a brief spurt of minor stardom years ago but hadn't had steady theater work since his wife, Rose, also an actor, died.

Delacourte had inherited wealth and had no job.

Cautious hope blossomed. If Delacourte had enough money not to have to work, that would give him the freedom to stalk his victims and the ability to spend a protracted amount of time with them. And an actor could disguise himself to look like anyone or no one. The man's wife's name had been Rose…

Why the hell had they never considered an actor before?

Jake's eyes quickly skimmed the rest of the profile. His gaze stopped abruptly and ice ran through his veins. The last play Delacourte had starred in was at a small dinner club in Durham, England. His role—Jack the Ripper.

Surging to his feet, Jake growled, "Got him."

McCall was beside him in a second and quickly scanned the screen. "Damn, that fits." Punching a number on his cellphone, he held it to his ear and said, "Deidre, find out as much as you can about an actor named Derrick Delacourte. Houses, properties…anything."

Not ready to assume anything, Jake forced himself to sit down again and continue his search. If Delacourte wasn't their guy, then the bastard had to be here somewhere.

Time slogged in slow motion. Jake continued to click on profile after profile, nothing else seemed to fit. Where the hell was Deidre? Why hadn't she called? Even as a small voice told him that it took time to do research, another voice snarled that Angela didn't have time. They needed information. Now.

A cellphone blared.

McCall answered, "What'd you find out?"

Jake watched his face. Dammit, never had he resented not being able to read the man's expression more than he did as this moment. Why didn't—

"Deidre," McCall said, "I'm putting you on speaker phone. Repeat what you just told me."

In a no-nonsense tone, completely different from her usual cheerful voice, Deidre said, "Delacourte owns a house outside London. As soon as I found the address, I called our Scotland Yard contact. Just received a call back. The police stormed the house and found what they're calling a torture chamber in the basement."

"Anything else?"

"They also found clothing and identification for two of the victims."

"No sign of Delacourte?"

"No. They said the mail and newspapers are all stacked up."

"What about other properties? Does he own any other houses?" Jake asked.

"Not that we can find. This was his family's home that he inherited."

"What about relatives?" McCall said. "There's got to be somebody who knows the guy."

"No relatives either. Even the neighbors don't know anything about him. Said he keeps to himself."

Jake turned away. Dammit, they'd identified the bastard only to have no idea where he was or what he had done with Angela.

"What about Clarissa Eaton?" McCall asked.

"So far, her body hasn't been found."

"Okay. Good work, Deidre. If you find anything else, let us—"

"Wait," Jake twisted back around. "Deidre, can you get a list of all the roles Delacourte's played?"

"Yes, I should be able to do that."

Jake looked at McCall. "The way he displays his victims.... What if he's playing a role and looking for a leading lady?"

"Could be. The roses...his wife's name was Rose. Maybe he's subliminally trying to bring back his dead wife."

Jake had a stomach churning thought. "And what's going to happen when he realizes Angela isn't his wife?"

McCall didn't speak but Jake saw the answer in his eyes. He was going to do to Angela the same thing he had done to the other women he had abducted.

"Okay, got them," a female voice interrupted their dark discussion.

While they'd been talking, Deidre had been working.

"Looks like he's played a lot of different roles. Almost a hundred. He—"

"What was his most successful role?" Jake said. "The one that gave him the most acclaim?"

"Looks like he got the best reviews from a play called The Last Man."

"And his character's name?"

"Richard Middlebrook." A pause. "Hold on a minute. Let me check..." Several more seconds of silence followed.

Jake couldn't breathe, could barely keep himself from dashing out the door. To where, he didn't know. Hell, hell, hell, come on, come on—

Deidre's excited voice broke into his cursing prayer. "A man named Richard Middlebrook rented a house in Reims a few days ago."

As Deidre rattled off the address, Jake pulled his Glock from his side holster and double-checked the magazine. They would go in with a battering ram if they could but if the rescue required subtlety, he'd be prepared.

McCall pocketed his cellphone, a triumphant gleam in his eyes. "That's a seven-minute drive from here."

Jake was opening the door before McCall finished. "Let's go."

The cement slab was hard and cold beneath her. Pain flowed through her body in an unending wave. How long had she been here? Hours, days? Weeks? Every time she regained some semblance of reasoning, he returned to her again. To torture, taunt, and shout odd, obscure directions she had no hope of understanding. Then he would shove papers in front of her and demand she read them aloud. She'd barely been able to make out the words, much less speak them. Would this agony never end?

She had long ago given up that LCR could save her. What had happened to Clarissa? The last time Angela had seen her, the woman was being rolled away on what looked like a hospital gurney. Though tied up and her mouth taped, Clarissa had twisted her head and given Angela a look—one of betrayal. Angela had told her she would save her and had broken her promise.

How could she have thought she could do this? Self-confidence had always been one of her best assets—seeing her through some of her darkest days. With all the naivety of a clueless child, she had carried that confidence into her first LCR mission. And now she faced the awful truth. Self-confidence hadn't gotten her into this plight, it had been blind arrogance. She had been so damn cocky, so very sure that her training combined with her intelligence and courage could conquer anything. Having dreamed of being an operative for so long, she had believed that all she'd needed was the opportunity. And now Clarissa Eaton would pay for that arrogance with her life. As would Angela.

"Welcome back."

Had he been standing there all along? Watching what remained of her spirit wither away? Waiting until he saw complete hopelessness before he began again?

Thousands of tiny jackhammers were on full blast inside her head and every part of her body, especially her feet, hurt with an unending agony. Ever since the hit on the head, her vision had been less than ideal. She had a concussion, at the least. That was only a minor problem though. And while pain covered every inch of her body, that wasn't her biggest issue, either. Her greatest problem was deep within her, where the real Angela lived, breathed, and had learned to survive no matter what. The damage there was irreparable. The unquenchable fire that sustained her had been doused. She had lost all hope.

Angela swallowed or tried to—there was nothing to swallow. Her mouth was completely void of moisture. She managed a weak, rasping, "Where's Clarissa?"

"She's resting for her finale."

"Finale?"

Smile smug, eyes gleaming with triumph, he said, "Yes, her time here is almost at an end."

With lightning speed, the fire she had thought dead reignited within her. White-hot fury zoomed like a rocket blast…washing, cleansing, renewing. Doubts and recriminations vanished. A new, brighter confidence took hold. No way in hell was this sadistic SOB going to win. No. Way. In. Hell.

"Need to go to the bathroom."

"Now, now. Is that the way I taught you to ask?"

Oh yes, she knew exactly what to say. Those words had been drilled into her with heartless regularity. She had no trouble obeying; she would do what she had to do, say what she had to say, to get free. "I'm begging you, my love. Please, may I attend to some personal needs?"

Delight lit up his features. "Excellent, my dear. I knew you would come around. And yes, I will grant your wish."

Her arms were always the most painful part of the freeing process. He unhooked the chains and lowered her arms gently to her side. "Wrap them around yourself like I taught you." When she complied, he said softly, "There you go."

Having him free her like this was painful for another reason. He was at his most gentle. Somehow this show of tenderness revolted her just as much or more than what he did to her when he was at his most sadistic.

As she dealt with the pain in her arms, he unlocked the chain at her feet. She was cuffed at her ankles, so even if she got free, she wouldn't be able to run fast or far. He had planned this well. It didn't matter. This would be her last attempt. If she failed…No, she refused to even finish that sentence in her mind. She would not fail. She had someone depending upon her. She had to save Clarissa and she had to save herself. She had too much to live for. Jake's harshly handsome face came to her mind. She wanted to see him again, tell him that she loved him. It didn't matter that he didn't love her. When you loved someone, you admitted that love. You didn't hold it inside you. Love was for giving away, not keeping.

He lifted her into his arms and carried her toward the bathroom. Usually when he did this, she was so weak or in such pain, she could barely function. And though she felt only slightly more coherent this time, it was now or never.

At the bathroom door, he paused to open it and for one split second, wasn't focused on her. Angela acted. Linking her hands together to form one giant fist, she swung around and up, smashing into the bastard's face. A satisfying crunch followed. Before he could react, she repeated the action.

Screaming his rage, he dumped her onto the floor and backed away, holding his bloodied, broken nose with his hands. Angela leaped to her feet. Ignoring all pain, she did what she had been longing to do for days. She took four hops—she had counted exactly how many it would take—and grabbed an axe that hung from the wall. Swinging it around, she slammed it toward where he should be standing. He wasn't there.

Pain erupted in her jaw, her neck jerked back. Adrenaline and determination kept her upright. She whirled around. He had somehow gotten behind her. With a wild animal roar, she swung the axe again and watched in triumph as it slammed into his head. The impact sounded like the thudding crack of a ripe melon.

His eyes were wide, filled with surprise and bewilderment. He took a step toward her. Angela raised the axe again. Before she could strike, he toppled like a felled tree, landing face-first onto the floor.

Dead or just unconscious? Didn't matter. She refused to take any chances. She carefully swung the axe, breaking the chains at her ankles. Turning, she then rushed back to her stone pallet and grabbed the chains he had used on her wrists. In seconds, she had him chained. Tugging with an inhuman strength that she knew was pure adrenaline, she dragged him to an old steel furnace, wrapped the chains around it and clicked the lock.

For the first time since this ordeal began, she drew in an easy breath.

Still she couldn't relax until she found Clarissa.

She turned and hobbled painfully, gratefully away from the creature on the floor. She went through the door and stood in a dreary hallway, noting several closed doors on each side.

"Clarissa?" she shouted. "Where are you?" Holding her breath, Angela listened. No sounds. Undeterred, she opened every door and peered inside—still no Clarissa. Despair filled her. He had lied to her—why had she believed he told the truth? Clarissa was already dead. Oh God, she had failed after all.

A soft, muffled noise hit her ears. Angela held her breath again. Yes, there it was. A voice…saying her name…coming from beneath her. Frantic, her eyes scanned the narrow hallway once more. There, in the shadows. Were those steps? Yes!

As if she had wings instead of badly damaged feet, she flew down the steps and into a small room, similar to the one she had just escaped. Clarissa lay on the gurney, chained. But her eyes were open and she was very much alive.

Swallowing a sob of thanksgiving, Angela ran to her and embraced her, chains and all.

"Oh, thank God. I thought you were dead," Clarissa said.

"I feared the same thing about you."

Clarissa looked fearfully behind Angela, as if the fiend might show up at anytime. “Where is he?”

“Chained to the radiator. Dead or just unconscious, I’m not sure…but he can’t get loose”

“Really?” Hope gleamed in Clarissa’s eyes. “I can’t believe this is over.”

“I need to find a phone.”

“I think there’s one in the room above this one. I heard it ring once.”

Angela rattled the chains on the gurney. “Do you know where the keys to these things are?”

“Behind you, hanging from that peg.”

Spotting them, she grabbed them and quickly unlocked the chains. Clarissa sat up slowly, tears flowing down her face. “I can’t believe I’m free.”

Angela held out her hand. “Let’s go make the call together. I’m not letting you out of my sight until we’re out of here.”

Clarissa dropped her feet to the floor, looked down and then gasped.

“What’s wrong? Are you hurt?”

Horror on her face, Clarissa whispered, “What happened to your feet?”

Agony shot through her, a reminder that she had some major injuries to deal with. She refused to look down. If she didn’t see the damage, she could continue to deny what he had done to her. “Never mind. Let’s go.”

Hand in hand, they walked up the steps together to make the call, ending their nightmare at last.

Jake’s cellphone rang. Pulling it from his pocket, assuming it was an LCR operative or one of the detectives, he answered, “Mallory.”

“Jake?”

He stopped breathing. Could it be? “Angela?”

McCall stiffened beside him and threw him a look of incredulity.

“Oh Jake.” Her voice was hoarse, barely above a whisper but it was definitely Angela.

"My God, are you all right?" He barely knew what to ask.

"I've been better. I'm not really sure where I am. Can you have this call traced? The monster's name is Derrick Delacourte."

"Where's Delacourte now?"

"He's unconscious and chained to a radiator in the basement. Where are you?"

He looked up at an ivy-covered brick mansion. "Right outside his house." Before the vehicle came to a stop, Jake was out of the car and running.

***

Jake was here? Outside the house? It took every ounce of self-control for Angela not to try to make it to the door. Since she would have had to crawl, she decided against it. Besides, her energy reserves were depleted. While she was making the call to Jake, Clarissa had found a raincoat hanging from the peg. And in the coat was the man's wallet, identifying him as Derrick Delacourte.

And now she was completely spent. Just the simple acts of making the phone call and putting the raincoat on had exhausted her. Both she and Clarissa sat at the bottom of the stairs, waiting.

They heard the door burst open and then Angela heard the most beautiful sound imaginable. "Angela! Where are you?"

"Down here," she shouted.

Running footsteps headed toward her and then, larger than life, Jake was there. Myriad emotions crossed his face as he reached for her. Unable to stop herself, she tried to stand, lost her balance and fell into his arms. In Jake's strong embrace, hearing his whispered words of thanksgiving, Angela finally gave herself permission to let go. With a sigh, she closed her eyes and allowed darkness to swallow her one last time.

# Chapter Nineteen

Guilt clawed his insides like a rabid wolf in a feeding frenzy. God in heaven, she had been tortured.

Jake leaned against the wall outside Angela's room. A doctor was with her. He had no real clue of her condition. Within a couple of minutes of finding her, an ambulance had arrived and whisked her away. She had still been unconscious but he had seen enough of her injuries to know that she had been through hell.

Clarissa Eaton appeared to be in much better shape, at least physically. Her only visible injuries were ligature bruises on her wrists and ankles plus severe dehydration. Mentally and emotionally she might never recover. She had gone into hysterics when Angela lost consciousness, shrieking and crying as if she were still in danger. McCall had managed to calm her down but she'd become hysterical again the instant the EMTs had placed her on a gurney.

The bastard was in the hospital too, under armed guard. He had briefly regained consciousness and claimed to know nothing about how the women had gotten into his home or what had happened to them.

Delacourte would be put away for life. That should be good enough, but it wasn't. Jake wanted him to suffer as much as those women had suffered. And he wanted to beat the ever-living shit out of the monster for what he had done to Angela.

The door opened beside him and two women walked out. One of the women, distinguished looking with gray hair and a slight limp, had the nametag with Dr. Lucia Bittner pinned to her white coat. The nurse standing beside her was middle-aged, stocky and reminded Jake a little of his grandmother. Both women wore the same dismal expressions on their faces.

"How is she?"

In lightly accented English, Dr. Bittner said, "Considering what she's been through, better than one would think. She has a concussion and multiple bruises all over her body. She also has some minor knife cuts to her torso that required a few stitches. Scarring should be minimal. Her feet are probably her most painful injuries. They have first-and second-degree burns, along with some shallow cuts. She won't be able to walk for several weeks."

Hell, the freak had only had her for two days but had apparently spent hours torturing her. Jake closed his eyes and swallowed back bile.

Dr. Bittner continued, "The tattoo can be removed but I would suggest she wait until her other injuries are healed."

"Tattoo?"

"Yes.

Confused, Jake shook his head. That was something Delacourte had never done before. "What kind of tattoo?"

"A rose. Unfortunately he wasn't a talented artist. It's quite crude."

"Where is it?"

"On the back of her neck."

He took in a shaky breath. Tattoos could be removed, burns would heal, scars would fade. But what about the inside where no one could see? What kind of psychological damage had the monster inflicted?

"Can I see her?"

"In a minute. A nurse is getting her more comfortable."

Jake nodded and thanked the doctor. Then slumping back against the wall, he covered his face with his hands and wept.

Angela opened her eyes, stretched gingerly and winced. She was still sore and despite the pain medication, her feet still hurt. But it was bearable. And, for the first time in days, her head was clear and her thoughts coherent. What a blessing.

A slight movement to her right brought her gaze to the man lying on the sofa against the wall. His six-foot-five frame was much too large for the short, uncomfortable looking piece of furniture. She had tried to get him to go back to his hotel room and he had refused. Other than when the doctors and nurses came in to perform their duties, Jake had been with her. She knew he had to be exhausted but he told her he wasn't leaving until she left. The tenderness in his eyes shut down her protests. She was definitely not going to complain if he wanted to stay with her.

At the sudden knocking at the door, Jake sprang to his feet. On his way across the room, he shot Angela a concerned, protective look—the same expression he'd had on his face since she'd woken in the hospital days ago. She had a feeling it was going to be some time before he let her out of his sight again.

He opened the door to reveal Noah, who entered carrying a tray of coffees in one hand and a box of pastries in the other. "Feel up to company?"

"Absolutely. I'm feeling much better today."

Noah passed her a coffee, then set the opened box of pasties on her tray table. After taking a long swallow of his coffee, he asked, "Samara get in touch with you?"

"Yes." Angela laughed and added, "Though it was hard to talk to her since Micah kept insisting on talking, too."

"He's been very worried about his Aunt Angela." His eyes went serious and sadder than she'd seen them in a long time. "We all have. Again, I'm sorry for what happened."

She shook her head. "I've told you, Noah, it wasn't your fault. Besides, it had a good ending."

She followed his gaze to her bandaged feet. "Okay, so not a perfect ending but a good one all the same. I'll heal. And we saved Clarissa and stopped Delacourte. That's what's most important."

"You're right, it is." He shot a glance at Jake. "I've got more info."

"What'd you find out?" Jake said.

"Delacourte was a working actor up until a few years ago when his one-man play folded. Before that, he had a small amount of success but mostly because of his wife, Rose. She was better known and apparently her husband rode his wife's coattails to semi-stardom. She died in a boating accident. After that, he had trouble getting work. His last gig—the one-man play—told the tale of Jack the Ripper. Apparently Delacourte identified with him in some way."

"With Rose being his wife's name and an actor who once played Jack the Ripper, seems like two damn big red flags we should've been able to detect."

Noah shrugged. "In hindsight, they are. I doubt anyone would have given them thought otherwise, even if they'd known. Until Angela told us, we had no idea he was using disguises. That information helped a helluva lot. Not too many people would've suspected a middle-aged has-been actor to be playing out his last role for real."

"I'm assuming the reason he chose tall, dark-haired women was because that's what Rose looked like?" Jake asked.

"You got it."

"But why did he take Clarissa?" Angela said. "Has anyone asked him?"

"He's still claiming to know nothing about any of the abductions or murders. The police faxed me a family portrait. Delacourte had an older sister who died when he was about fifteen. Looked a lot like Clarissa."

The conversation she'd had with Clarissa after she had been taken came back to her. "That fits," Angela said.

"What fits?" Jake said.

"Something Clarissa told me. I don't remember a lot of what she said because of the drug he'd given me, but I remember she said that he kept telling her the reason he had taken her would soon be revealed to him. He must've felt some sort of connection with her but in his crazed mind, he couldn't figure out why."

"Maybe that's why he never injured her," Jake said. "But why kill the women who looked like his wife?"

It was beginning to make sense in a sick twisted way. "I think he was trying to replace her," Angela answered. "That's why he kept shoving those scripts in my face and telling me to read. And when the women didn't live up to his expectations, he got rid of them and went on to another one." Her brow furrowed. "But why put the tattoo on my neck? He had never done that with any of his other victims."

Noah and Jake locked gazes, the expression on both men's faces indicated neither wanted to answer the question.

"What?" she asked.

"We think he had chosen to keep you," Jake said. "Marking you with the rose was his brand."

Despite her feeling of wellbeing, shudders of revulsion went through her. She tried her best to make light of the situation by quipping, "How about that. I must be a better actress than I thought."

Noah's mouth moved up in a slight smile but Jake's remained flat and grim.

Wanting to erase the sadness from his face, she changed the subject. "Did Clarissa make it home okay?"

"Yes." Noah's mouth tilted up even more. "She's tougher than she looks."

He was right. Clarissa had come by yesterday to thank Angela once again. Though the young woman looked fragile and would probably suffer nightmares for years, the set to her chin and the look in her eyes told Angela she would be fine. Amazing what a person could endure and survive.

"I'm hoping I'll get to go home today."

Jake shook his head. "You need to stay here a couple more days."

"I'll feel better at home. There's nothing more the doctors can do. I just need some healing time."

"You can't walk yet."

She lifted her chin. "So? No matter if I stay here or go home, I won't be able to walk for weeks. At least if I'm home, I'll be in my own bed."

Jake watched her closely. Even though he wanted to keep her here, protected from the world, he didn't argue. Just seeing the stubborn light in her eyes was worth any additional worry he had that she needed to be completely healed before going home. Compared to how she'd looked three days ago, her recovery was nothing short of miraculous. He would never forget the moment she tried to walk to him and then collapsed in his arms. Her courage awed him.

He had yet to tell her that she wasn't going home alone. They hadn't talked about their relationship. Hell, she had no idea that he even wanted one. He had been waiting for the right time but now wondered why he hadn't already told her. At that question, he stopped. Of course he knew why he hadn't told her. What if she said no? She didn't seem to blame him for what happened but that didn't mean she wanted anything else to do with him. He'd rejected her, slept with her when she was in a vulnerable state, and almost let her get killed by a serial killer. It was a wonder she allowed him into her room.

Remaining cautious, he said, "Let's see what the doctor says before you get too set on leaving."

As if she'd been summoned, a knock sounded and Dr. Bittner appeared. "How are we doing today?"

"We're doing just great and want to go home."

She smiled. "Now that's a coincidence. I came to tell you that you're being released today."

Angela threw a look at Jake, her eyes dancing with an 'I told you so' light. How could she act as if nothing had happened when every time he closed his eyes, he imagined the horror she had endured? Her resilience amazed and humbled him.

"No trying to walk on those feet for at least another ten days or so. I'll send your chart to your regular physician."

Jake listened carefully as the doctor issued orders about her feet, the lingering headaches she might experience because of her concussion, and the need to watch for infection of the numerous cuts on her body.

"I was thinking about hiring a nurse," Angela said. "Just for a few days to help me get in and out of the shower and things like that."

The doctor nodded approvingly. "That's an excellent idea."

Jake could feel McCall's eyes on him. Yesterday he had informed his boss that he would be taking care of Angela when she was released. The man had been set on bringing Angela to his home and hiring someone to care for her. He'd said Samara was quite intent on the idea. Jake had assured him that Samara was more than welcome to come by for visits but that Jake would see to Angela's care.

McCall hadn't argued but had seemed damned amused for some reason.

"I have the plane on standby," McCall said. "I'll let them know we'll be leaving in a few hours."

As soon as McCall and the doctor walked out the door, Jake turned to her. "I'm going home with you."

She blinked at him. "Of course you are. There's plenty of room on the plane."

"No, I mean I'm moving in with you."

"What?"

He grinned, hoping he didn't look as nervous as he felt. "You told me I needed to find a better place to live."

"Do I get a say in this?"

Jake swallowed hard, the lump in his throat growing larger. Dammit, she was right. After what happened to her, she probably wanted nothing to do with him.

"Let me do this for you, Angela. What happened to you was my fault. I should have watched your back."

Dark eyes stared hard at him for several seconds. He withstood the look. If she wanted to slug him for not being there for her, he'd take that, too. It was no less than he deserved.

Finally, with a small nod, she said, "I appreciate the offer. I could really use the help."

Relieved that she hadn't just told him to get the hell out of her life, he said, "I appreciate you letting me help."

"You're wrong about one thing, Jake. What happened wasn't your fault."

He disagreed, but wasn't going to argue. She'd let him off the hook way too easy. "I can't believe you're healing so quickly. You'll be back to researching at LCR before you know it."

Instead of the spunky comeback he expected, her eyes remained dark and solemn. Jake didn't know what to say to return the light to her eyes. He only knew that he felt responsible for being the one to make it go away in the first place.

# Chapter Twenty

*Paris*

"This tea is too tepid," Angela groused.

"Sorry." Jake took back the mug of tea he'd just handed her. "Let me heat it up for you."

She watched him disappear into the kitchen and blew out a heavy sigh. There was absolutely nothing wrong with the tea. It was Jake's attitude that was driving her crazy.

She'd been home for over a week. Since her apartment was on the third floor, she had decided to stay in her parents' home. A single level with no steps or stairs, the house was a breeze to maneuver through on her crutches.

Oddly enough, coming to her parents' home had given her some kind of closure. The grief wasn't as sharp or overwhelming as it had been before. Instead she had found comfort here, as if her family's love had been retained within these walls. She now knew she wouldn't be selling the house. She was going to give up her apartment and move back here. This was her home now.

Hearing the microwave ding, Angela braced herself for the confrontation. Jake had taken care of every need she might have. He'd been sweet, attentive and kind. Had done everything she asked and had attempted to anticipate her needs before she even had them. Was it any wonder he was driving her up the wall?

Where was the man who went out of his way to piss her off to get a reaction? Where was the man who joked with her, flirted with her? Where was the man who'd made such passionate love to her that just the memory of that night could bring her to arousal?

She missed that man. The fascinating, frustrating, and infinitely lovable Jake Mallory had been replaced with a guilt-ridden, too-polite stranger. She wanted the real Jake Mallory back. She wanted to fight and laugh with him, kiss and caress him until her breath became his.

He blamed himself for what happened and had apologized multiple times. And for each apology, she had insisted that what happened hadn't been his fault. The guilt from his wife's tragic death had colored the true facts. He was intent on taking all the blame on himself. Angela couldn't allow that to continue.

And even if there was blame, then it should be shared. They'd been partners and had completely missed the fact that just because she had taken herself off the op, didn't mean the killer wasn't following her.

For the last couple of days she had become deliberately impossible, making all sorts of demands on him that any reasonable person would refuse. But Jake and his wrongly placed guilt continued to take her abuse. She wanted to cry.

Returning to stand in front of her, he handed her a steaming mug. "Here you go. See if it's any better."

Not lifting her hand to take the tea, she just shook her head. "It won't be."

"What?"

"Look Jake, I really appreciate all you've done but I don't think this is going to work out."

"Why?"

"Because nothing you do can change what happened."

Setting the tea on the table beside the couch, Jake slumped into a chair across from her. "You're right. God, I'm so sorry, Angela. Instead of bringing you tea, I should be asking your forgiveness. I should be—"

"No. Stop, Jake. I can't take it anymore."

"You want me to leave?"

"What I want you to do is acknowledge that what happened to me wasn't your fault."

"Of course it was. "

Frustrated, she went another direction. "What did you tell me when I first called and told you that the killer was within a few yards of me?"

He frowned. "I don't know what you mean."

"What did you tell me to do…what were your exact instructions?"

"I told you to hold your gun on him till I could get to you."

"Exactly. Did I do that? No. I disobeyed your order and I let Delacourte take me."

"But I shouldn't have allowed—"

"Allowed? You didn't have a choice. I made the decision on my own."

Several long moments of silence followed. Angela's heart was in her throat as she watched emotions play across Jake's face. Then slowly, as realization came, the too solemn expression she'd seen the last few days changed to the beginning of anger. His eyes took on a glint and her heart kicked up an optimistic beat. Had she, at last, penetrated his wrongly placed guilt?

"You had no right to make that decision on your own."

"But I did. And it turned out okay."

"It sure as hell didn't. You were tortured, dammit."

"But I'm alive, Jake. And so is Clarissa."

Jake surged to his feet and shoved his fingers through his hair. He'd been living on adrenaline since Angela was taken and had yet to let go. Now it all came crashing down on him—the fear, the dread, the terrible knowledge that she could be dead. And then finding her, only to realize that she had been tortured.

Now came the anger, which he had to admit felt damn good. "You disobeyed a direct order," he said softly.

"Yes, I did."

"You could've been killed."

"I know."

The more he thought about it, the more pissed he became. He paced as he continued, "You were a rookie. Making this decision against my orders was impulsive and irrational. Getting yourself killed wouldn't have solved anything." He whirled around to glare at her. "You should've followed my orders. That was what you agreed to do. You should have—"

For the first time since he'd begun lambasting her, he noticed that instead of looking guilty or angry, she was smiling.

"What the hell are you smiling about?"

"Because this is exactly what you should have said to me all along instead of treating me like some sort of damaged creature. I'm injured, not damaged. I can take the heat."

Explosive feelings he hadn't had in years coursed through him. Hell, he didn't know if he'd ever felt this way. His head told him to continue to rail at her, that he was still furious with her for putting herself at risk. His heart said something else.

Listening to his heart for the first time in years, Jake dropped to his knees in front of her and pulled her into his arms. Holding her tight, he whispered harshly, "Do you know what it would have done to me if I'd lost you?"

"I'm so sorry I put you through that." Her arms twined around his shoulders and she said softly, "Forgive me?"

His chest tight with emotions he dared not let loose, Jake pulled away slightly to kiss her. He had meant it to be soft and sweet…a loving kiss, nothing more. Making any demands on Angela's abused body was out of the question.

As usual, Angela had other ideas. The instant Jake's mouth touched hers, she opened, letting his tongue slip through. When he would have pulled away, she grabbed his shoulders and spoke against his lips, "I'm not made of glass."

Refusing to deepen the kiss, he backed away. "I took advantage of you once before."

Her responding laugh was soft and full of sexy confidence. "Really? Well then, feel free to take advantage of me like that any time you like. In fact, I have some time right now. How about you?"

Unable to stop himself, Jake ground his mouth against hers, smothering her laughter. As she melted into his arms, peaceful contentment filled him—something he barely recognized as belonging to him. With Angela in his arms, safe and sound, all was right with his world at last.

Lifting her into his arms, Jake headed to the bedroom he'd been using. Every night he had fantasized about having her there with him. He felt as though he'd waited a lifetime to show Angela what she meant to him. His body urged him to lay her on the bed and bury himself inside her until they were both breathless and sated. Again, he listened to his heart. The first time they'd been together, it had been all about heat and quenching the fire that had been building between them since they first met. And though the fire within him was hotter than ever, tonight he wanted to show her what she meant to him. She needed to understand that this wasn't just a brief, intense moment of passion. This was something more.

Jake settled her onto the bed and pulled away to look down at her. Never had she looked more beautiful to him. In his lifetime, he had seen his share of courage. He knew what bravery looked like and what it didn't. What Angela had survived was anyone's worst nightmare. And instead of being emotionally damaged, there was an odd kind of peace about her. As if the experience had uncovered a hidden depth of strength within her.

"What are you waiting for?"

With a quick jerk, Jake pulled his shirt apart, barely aware of the clicking noise as buttons hit the hardwood floor. Angela laughed softly at his apparent urgency... the husky sound pushing him to go even faster.

Next came his shoes, jeans and then his underwear. When he was completely nude, he came to her, aching and hard, so aroused that at one touch, he might explode. He wouldn't.

Kneeling beside her, he raised her to sit up. "Let's get rid of these clothes." His voice sounded like the growl of a hungry wolf—appropriate since that's exactly how he felt.

Her expression a mixture of curiosity and need, Angela sat up and looked expectantly at Jake. With quick efficiency, he stripped her bare.

"Wow, you're really good at getting clothes off fast."

Pushing her gently back onto the bed, he came over her. "Let me show you what else I'm really good at."

Breathless with anticipation, Angela lay supine on the bed, waiting for Jake's next move. She wanted to smooth her hands down his hard, muscular body and allow her mouth to follow. Reading his expression, she knew that this wasn't like their first time. Then it had been all about devouring each other to satisfy their need. This time, it was something altogether different. Hesitant to read too much into his tender expression, Angela nevertheless felt more hopeful than she ever had before with Jake.

Starting with the edge of her jaw, Jake's mouth glided down her skin. He hadn't shaved in a couple of days and the stubble was both abrasive and arousing. Angela arched her neck to give him greater access. Jake obliged, and then stopped at the hollow of her throat to press a tender, hot kiss.

"Jake," she whispered.

"Hmm?"

"Nothing. Just...Jake."

She could feel his smile against her skin. As he moved away from her neck, her nipples hardened in anticipation. When his hot mouth covered one, Angela's entire body arched in response.

Unable to resist, she weaved her hands through his hair and held his head as he suckled her. The throb of her sex coincided with every draw of his mouth. Her body arched again, needing his touch, wanting him.

A big hand pressed against her lower belly to still her movements. He was only inches away from the part that throbbed, needed, and literally ached for him. She tried shifting, hoping his fingers would slide down.

Jake released a husky, masculine laugh, causing delicious goose bumps to cover her body. "Impatient, are we?"

"Very," Angela gasped.

"Good things come to those who wait."

"I feel like I've been waiting a lifetime."

He raised his head, locked his gaze with hers, and answered quietly, "I do too."

Her heart soared at the declaration. Before she could respond, he moved swiftly and placed his mouth in the exact spot she needed him. Angela opened her legs, arched her hips, and gave herself up to the most intensely erotic moment of her life as Jake used his mouth and tongue…even his teeth to give her pleasure. She stiffened as she neared the edge. With each thrust of his tongue, she drew closer and closer to that moment where she knew she would fall into ecstasy. A blinding light flickered behind her lids and she was there, falling… falling and then she was suspended, floating… Her keening cry echoed through the house as she zoomed through space and then crash-landed into a soft, velvet oblivion.

Breathlessly, she raised her head to look at Jake. His eyes, a darker blue than she'd ever seen them, glittered with satisfaction. "Do you know how beautiful you are when you come?"

Angela, who never blushed, could feel her face heating. "Um…no."

He grinned and came over her, settling between her legs. Poised at her entrance, he said softly, "You will." And with that promise, he buried himself inside her.

Forgetting his astonishing statement, she wrapped her legs around his lean hips and gave herself over to Jake's delicious lovemaking. Where he had been tender and gentle before, this time it was hard, fast and exactly what she needed.

"Need more," Jake muttered.

"What?"

In an abrupt move, he pulled out of her and went to his knees. Before she could ask what was wrong, Jake hooked his arms under her knees, pushed her legs up and then spread them wider. Then he was in her again, going deeper than he ever had before. Pistoning back and forth, his erection rubbed frantically against her clit creating an erotic friction, sparking a fire that burned within her entire body. Urging him on with pleas that she barely comprehended, Angela found herself on a peak she'd never reached. Without thought of the consequences, only knowing she wanted Jake with her, she wrapped both hands around his hard length and pushed him even harder inside her.

A sound like the growl of a rabid animal emerged from Jake's chest and he slammed into her. Biting her lip to hold on to the ecstasy as long as possible, she closed her eyes. How she loved this rougher, out of control side of Jake.

"Open your eyes."

Her eyelids flickered opened and she gasped. She had seen Jake aroused before but the heated intensity of his gaze was nothing compared to this. He was a man teetering on the edge.

He ground out between clenched teeth, "We do this together. Eyes wide open."

She nodded.

Their gazes locked, Jake plunged again and then again, once more pistoning inside. Her clit so aroused it was exquisitely painful, she looked deep into his eyes and when they exploded together, she gasped out the words she had been longing to say for so long, "I love you, Jake Mallory."

And then the world disappeared.

Rolling to his side, Jake propped himself on his elbow and took in the panting, sweat- slick, slender body beside him. Dammit, he'd meant to be easy with her, wanting to show her how much she meant to him. Angela had been through hell and he'd just pounded into her with all the finesse of a horny gorilla.

"Are you all right?" she asked breathlessly.

He jerked at the question. "Hell, I'm the one who should be asking you that. I'm sorry I was so rough. I—"

Her fingers on his lips stopped him from finishing. "Oh no you don't. If you apologize for the best, most sexually intense moment of my life, I'll—"

Feeling only slightly better, Jake's mouth curved slightly. "You'll what?"

"I'll cook for you."

He barked out a laugh. "Is that supposed to be a threat?"

"You've never tasted my cooking."

Gathering her close, he buried his face against her neck and breathed in the delicious fragrance that was Angela. "I am sorry I wasn't more gentle. When you, uh, grabbed me, I kind of lost it." He winced. Blaming her for his loss of control was particularly assholish. "Not that that's an excuse."

He felt her head shake. "Lose it with me any time you like. Okay?"

A giant breath huffed from his chest and he raised his head to face her, needing to say something before they went any further. "What you said…about loving me. Was that in the heat of the moment or did you—"

"I meant it. I've loved you forever."

He cleared his throat. "I haven't said those words to a woman since I lost Teresa."

Instead of asking for them, she shook her head. "I don't need them."

Hell, he wanted to be able to say them but she deserved more than token words. He tried to explain, "I swore when I lost Teresa, I'd never let myself be vulnerable like that again. Loving someone means opening yourself. I closed down after she died. I don't know that I can ever go that far again. But I do want a future with you…that is, if you're not too pissed."

"Jake, you don't have to say them. And yes, I want a future with you, too."

Relieved that she understood and wasn't expecting more than he could give, he pulled her back into his arms and began to make love to her again, determined that this time, he would show her the gentleness he had intended before. As he kissed and caressed her, lingering tenderly over the areas where she had been cut or bruised, he shut down a voice inside his head. The one that mockingly told him it was too late to worry about falling in love. That the feeling was already there, whether he was ready to deal with it or not.

# CHAPTER TWENTY-ONE

Two weeks later and Angela was still experiencing bliss. Jake might not be able to say the words 'I love you' yet but not a day went by that he didn't show her how much he cared. Romantic gifts like flowers, candy, takeout from a favorite restaurant, a book she had mentioned wanting to read were all wonderful and much appreciated. The practical things were just as special, like repairing a stopped-up shower drain or adding a brighter bulb in her reading lamp. He'd also helped pack up some of her family's things for storage, then held her while she cried once again for them.

He spoiled and cosseted her, treating her as if she were the most important person in the world to him. Angela didn't need the words. Jake's actions told her more than enough.

Not a night went by that they didn't make love. She loved his tender, gentle lovemaking. He would kiss her all over, taking his time with her, until she was so aroused she was almost screaming with need. When she was to the point where she barely knew her own name, he would slide into her and they'd fall into oblivion together.

She also adored his wilder side—watching him lose that famous control was an incredible turn-on. He went after his pleasure like he was starving for her. It wasn't until she performed an erotic striptease for him that she saw that side of him again. After they had recovered, he had fulfilled his promise and had her stand in front of a full-length mirror while he stood behind her and made her come with his fingers. They'd both watched as she climaxed. Even though she had blushed the entire time, she had almost passed out from the pleasure.

Once she was able to get around without her crutches, Jake returned to work but came home to her each night. She knew there were longer, out-of-town jobs he could have taken and didn't because of her.

She should have realized the idyllic time wouldn't last. What they'd experienced wasn't the real world. It had been almost honeymoonish—too good to be true. But when gritty reality raised its ugly head and ensnared them in its nasty claw, Angela never saw it coming.

The day began as perfect as all the others. She had a consultation appointment with a plastic surgeon to have the rose tattoo removed. She hadn't even realized it was there until Dr. Bittner mentioned it when she was examining her. Apparently Delacourte had applied the tat during one of the many times she'd been unconscious. When she had seen what the fiend had done, she had been determined to rid herself of the ugly reminder of her experience.

Dr. Goldstein, the plastic surgeon, inadvertently changed her mind.

After examining the tat and assuring her it could be removed with minimal scarring, he'd asked how she'd gotten it. Angela had given him a condensed version of events. Dr. Goldstein had nodded his head approvingly. "You're a survivor."

She had walked out of the doctor's office with a new perspective. The instant she was in the car, she had instructed Jake to take her to a talented tattoo artist she knew. Marcel had been horrified at the ugly tat and promised to turn it into a work of art. He succeeded beyond her expectations. Two hours later, she had walked out of the building with a beautiful rose in full bloom and in the middle of the flower was the word: *Survivor.*

Even Jake, who'd been shocked to learn what she was going to do, said it was beautiful.

After that, the day had only gotten better. They'd eaten a late lunch at one of her favorite restaurants. Jake ordered a bottle of wine and they had laughed and talked like they didn't have a care in the world.

When they returned home, they'd fallen into each other's arms, ravishing each other as if it had been days and not hours since they'd made love. The perfect ending to a perfect day.

It was late that evening when everything blew up in her face. They were sitting in front of the fire, drinking wine and relaxing when Angela made the announcement that changed her world once again. "I'm going back to work next week."

Jake had been playing with her hair, smoothing it behind her ear. His mouth turned up in a small smile. "That's good to hear. I figured you'd want to get back soon. As busy as you like to be, you've probably been bored stiff these last few weeks."

"Absolutely not. This time with you was wonderful but I'm feeling fabulous now and I'm completely healed. There's no reason I can't work."

"I've missed seeing you there. Deidre's a sweetheart but when I walk in, I expect to see your beautiful face. I'm always disappointed when I don't."

"Noah said she's doing a great job."

"She really came through for us on Delacourte. You trained her well. Having two brilliant researchers instead of one is only better for LCR."

When her body went stiff, Jake looked down at her. "What's wrong?"

Angela hesitated. For obvious reasons, they hadn't discussed the future. When existing in a bubble, concentrating on the here and now, things like what would happen when she returned to work were pushed aside. But now, it had to be addressed. He hadn't been onboard at the beginning when he first learned she wanted to be an operative. Surely, after everything that had happened, his opinion had changed.

"I'm not going back as a researcher. I'm going back as a field operative."

His face as forbidding as a dark thundercloud, he shook his head. "No, you're not. You told Noah you quit. That you wanted to go back to research."

"That was before. Now that I know I can handle myself, it's what I still want to do."

"Dammit, did almost dying not teach you anything?"

"Yes, it taught me how strong and resilient I am. Delacourte tried to destroy the essence of who I am—it didn't work. I admit, I was arrogant early on…I've lost the arrogance and now have something stronger in its place. I know I can handle myself when crunch time comes. I will be a damn good operative. I know I need additional training to overcome some issues and Noah's already told me he'll only give me assignments he thinks I can handle until I prove myself."

"You've already talked to McCall about this?"

"Yes. Yesterday."

Surprisingly, or maybe not surprisingly, since Noah often seemed to have an inside view of people's thoughts, he hadn't acted shocked when she had told him she still wanted to be an operative. She had listened to his list of expectations and had agreed to every one of them. She would do whatever was necessary to become the kind of operative she'd always dreamed.

Jake couldn't stop shaking his head. How the hell had he not seen this coming? How did she not know where he stood?

"We've got something good here, Angela. I assumed you felt the same way."

"Of course I do."

The confusion on her face told him she didn't understand how their relationship and her job were related. In his mind, they were so intertwined that separation wasn't possible.

"Then, if you feel that way, why the hell would you even consider going back as an operative?"

"Aren't you an operative?"

"Of course. It's my job."

"And my job, too."

"No, it's not, dammit. You're a researcher." He stopped and tried something else. "Look, I admit, you're talented—your skills are top-notch. But LCR has over a hundred operatives. We only have a handful of researchers. You have nothing to prove to anyone by going back into the field."

"This is the very same argument you gave when you first learned I wanted to be an operative. I understood it then because you didn't know what I was capable of. Now that you know, why would you think I'd want to go back to being a researcher?"

"Because it almost got you killed."

"All operatives live with that knowledge daily. But I took down a serial killer single-handedly. I saved Clarissa's life, my own, and who knows how many others. You're dismissing it as if it meant nothing."

"I'm not dismissing it at all. What you did was damn brave but that…" He pulled in a deep breath and tried again. "What I'm saying is..."

Jake stopped. He was stumbling all over himself to come up with a better way to say what he was feeling. But what the hell…she had to know where he stood. "When I lost Teresa, it almost killed me. When I thought I'd lost you, I wanted to die. I can't go through that again. I won't."

"Jake, in all the years I've been with LCR, we've lost exactly one operative. Those are damn good odds."

Her bright, beautiful smile was supposed to reassure him but all he saw was how she had looked when he'd found her at Delacourte's house of horrors. He couldn't bear to see her like that again or have something even worse happen to her.

"Whether there have been no deaths or fifty doesn't matter. Knowing you're going through danger day after day isn't something I can live with. Period."

Dark brown eyes, filled with hurt and confusion, stared at him for the longest. Putting down an ultimatum was probably a dumbass thing to do but he wasn't going to lie to her. This had to be said.

She stood, wrapped her arms around herself, and said the very words he had been thinking, "So what you're saying is, if I go back as an operative, we're through?"

Even as his heart twisted at the thought of never being with her again, she had to know the consequences of her decision. "That's exactly what I'm saying."

Turning away from him, Angela bit her lip to keep it from trembling. Out of all the directions she anticipated this conversation going, this hadn't been on her radar. She had stupidly assumed she had proven herself to him.

In a voice thick with emotion, she confessed softly, "I fell in love with you almost from the moment we met. I already knew about you and what you had endured, but when I saw you, it was cemented in my mind—I knew I would love you forever." She whirled back around to face him. "Not once did I consider not loving you or wanting to be with you because of your job. Even now, knowing I could lose you on an op, I would never consider asking you to stop doing something that you loved. And yet, that's exactly what you're asking of me."

"Dammit, you're acting as though I have no reason for my fears. I almost lost you. Can you not see why I would feel this way?"

"Yes, I can understand your feelings. But here's the thing. My family went to visit some friends for the weekend and died in a freak accident. Death and tragedy can occur on any given day for anyone, LCR operative or civilian. Not being an operative won't necessarily keep me from dying."

"No, but as a researcher, you have a better chance of living a long life. At least you wouldn't be putting yourself at risk every day."

Releasing a shaky breath, searching for a calm within the storm of her emotions, she stated her position: "I'm not a researcher anymore, I'm an operative. I love you Jake, but I would never ask you to be something you're not."

He snorted. "You were an operative for barely two weeks."

"I've wanted to be an operative for years." She glared at him as she added, "And don't you dare diminish what I accomplished."

"I'm not. I'm just pointing out that being something for two weeks doesn't exactly make it a career."

"It does when it's all I ever wanted to do. And it's what I intend to do for years to come."

They glared silently at each other for several seconds. Angela wanted to throw her arms around him and plead with him to understand. She wouldn't. He had to come to the realization on his own, without her trying to seduce him into accepting her decision.

She watched helplessly, hopelessly, as Jake whirled, jerked up his jacket and headed for the front door.

"Where are you going?"

"I'm leaving. I'll come back for my things later."

"So that's it. It's either my dream or you."

He opened the door and then stopped. Turning back to her, he said, "I thought I was your dream. Coming in second place sucks."

The door slammed, putting an end to her future with Jake and breaking her heart in the process.

# CHAPTER TWENTY-TWO

*One month later*

*Agar, France*

"The bastard's got to be coming down soon," Aidan growled. "He's been like that for hours."

"Whatever he's taken, I hope to hell he's enjoying himself," Seth responded.

Stooped behind a jumble of bushes, Angela adjusted her earbud. A few hours ago, Aidan and Seth had been ready to storm the house where Rupert Gardon was holding his wife and children hostage. Because of the sensitivity of the case—Rupert was the son of a prominent politician in Agar—LCR had been called in to do a quiet snatch and grab.

Things hadn't gone as planned. Rupert was, as Seth so succinctly put it, loaded for bear. An AK-47 was strapped to his shoulder while he held a Glock securely in his hand. Even crazier, Seth had spotted several sticks of dynamite lying on the kitchen table. The man had enough explosives to incinerate the house and everyone inside it. And to make matters a thousand times more dangerous, he was apparently hyped up on some kind of drug. He had been pacing back and forth on the front porch for hours without a break. And though they had yet to see anyone else, they had strong suspicions that Rupert had brought some friends of his along.

LCR had expected a simple rescue operation and Rupert was prepared for Armageddon.

After conferring with Aidan and Angela, Seth had made the call to Noah, requesting more operatives. Until reinforcements arrived, the three of them were to watch and wait.

This was her fourth op since returning to work. As usual, Noah had been true to his word—only giving her assignments where the danger was minimal or partnering her with some of his most experienced people. She'd barely broken a sweat on any of them but Angela wasn't complaining. Noah had warned her that her assignments would be heavily supervised for a while. He had severe regret for allowing her to take the Red Rose Killer assignment. Angela couldn't blame him for his caution. She had rushed things and they had all paid a heavy price.

She wouldn't wish her experience with Delacourte on anyone but she had learned some valuable lessons. Jake's words that his Army chaplain gave him had proven true. When the time came, God had given her courage to act. She hadn't done anything superhuman but she had taken down a serial killer and saved Clarissa Eaton's life, as well as her own. And she'd proven to herself that she could step up and be an effective operative.

She hadn't heard from Jake since he'd stormed out the door. He was on assignment in the States. She didn't know when the op would end or when he would return to Paris. His desertion hurt. And the loneliness of her bed was unbearable at times. More than once she had picked up the phone to call him and promise anything if he would just come back. She hadn't made that call and she wouldn't. Yes, she loved him but he was asking her to be someone she wasn't. If she agreed to his demands, how long would it be before she began to resent his ultimatum?

The adage her mother used to say came to her mind—cutting off your nose to spite your face. She wanted to be with Jake—she loved him, ached for him. Every night when she closed her eyes, the memories of what they had shared crashed over her. Did Jake miss her as much as she missed him?

How would he treat her when he came home? After what they'd shared, she couldn't go back to the lighthearted flirting they'd had before. Nor could she bear the painful awkwardness that came from a relationship gone bad. What if he ignored her altogether? Just acted as if she didn't exist? That would be even more hurtful.

"Okay…listen up," Seth said. "Our reinforcements are here. Thorne, Montgomery and I will go through the front. Ingram and Kelly, go through the back. Everyone else, stay out of sight but close. We still have no idea how many are inside. If they start swarming like pissed-off wasps, be ready."

Angela tensed, waiting for the raid to begin. How many additional operatives had Noah sent? She smiled to herself. Rupert and his friends were in for a big surprise.

"Let's do this," Seth said.

Staying low, Angela moved closer to the house and hid behind a large stone well in the middle of the yard. Using her binoculars, she watched as Riley and Justin sneaked in through the back door. She couldn't see them but knew that Seth, Aidan and Jordan were going in the front just as silently.

Though all LCR missions required being armed, no one had intended to use lethal force. Rupert's weapons and obvious instability had changed the game. Now, in addition to a rescue, Rupert and his friends had to be neutralized before anyone got hurt.

Adrenaline flowed through her. Expecting anything, she waited. What she heard next chilled her blood ice cold.

"Shit!"

"Ah dammit, what the hell…!"

"Go get him!"

A barrage of gunfire blasted, the shots so loud in her ear, she winced. Shouts, screams and curses erupted. Her gun steady in her hand, Angela held her position. Though everything within her wanted to rush inside and see if she could help, she waited. They all had jobs to do. If she was needed, they would let her know.

She heard a door squeak open and detected movement at the back of the house. Pointing her binoculars to where the sound came from, she squinted, focused, and then went stiff with dread. *Oh hell.*

Running like a man possessed, Jake headed to the back of the house. He'd been stationed at a side window and saw what was about to go down. If he didn't get there in time, he knew who would be facing the maniac that came out the door.

He skidded to a stop and froze in place. If he moved, it would cause a distraction. And if that happened, Angela and the woman they had come to rescue would be blown to pieces.

"Rupert," Angela said softly, "you don't want to do this."

"Oh, but I do. She has defied me for the last time. She will pay the price for her disobedience."

"And your children? What's to become of them? Their mother will be gone and their father in prison."

Rupert snorted. "My father is a very important man. He will make all of this disappear as if it never happened. And believe me, my children will be much better off. I'll find them a mother who is loyal."

"And will you kill her too if she doesn't obey your commands?"

*Easy, baby,* Jake thought. Piss Rupert off and there was no telling what the unpredictable idiot would do. Beatrice Gardon stood eight feet in front of her husband, a homemade bomb of dynamite strapped to her torso. Rupert held a Glock in one hand and what looked like a garage door opener he was using as a detonator in the other. It would be no problem for him to press the button for the bomb and squeeze off a bullet simultaneously.

Angela stood between Rupert and his wife. Both the bomb and the gun were a danger to her.

"If a woman makes a vow, then she should keep it," Rupert snarled. "She promised to obey me and she didn't."

"Rupert," Beatrice sobbed, "I'll do what you ask, I promise. Just please don't do this."

Rupert lifted both hands. "Your promises come too late, woman."

His heart in his throat, Jake took off. The only option was to tackle the man before he pressed the detonator or squeezed the trigger. Before he could get to

Gardon, Angela did something extraordinary. Almost a blur, her movements so swift, she knocked Gardon's gun from his hand with her forearm and kicked the bomb detonator out of his other hand. Then, before Jake could make a grab for it, she caught the detonator in mid-air.

With a soft cry, Beatrice Gardon's knees gave out. Switching directions, Jake dove forward and caught the terrified woman in his arms. He turned back to check on Angela and was unsurprised to see that she had Rupert face down on the ground. Kneeling on top of the man's back, she was already cuffing his wrists with zip-ties.

"Now that, sweetheart, was impressive," Jake said.

She twisted her head around to face him. "Jake? What are you doing here?"

He wanted to grin, tell her how damn proud he was of her. He wanted to throw her over his shoulder and take her away from the danger. However, there was still the small issue of a bomb attached to the poor sobbing woman in his arms. Jake examined the device. Thankfully it was as crude as it was ugly—a simple wire/switch combo. He jerked the wire connector, unbuckled the vest and lifted the dynamite off.

The instant he did that, kids were shrieking around him, screaming, "Mama! Mama!"

Jake moved quietly out the way and glanced over at Angela. Instead of looking at him, her eyes were on the reunion of mother and children.

An uncomfortable lump in his throat, Jake stood, transfixed. He knew he would never forget this moment. Triumph and satisfaction had turned Angela from beautiful to something otherworldly. A transformation was taking place before him. Angela Delvecchio, survivor and one incredibly strong woman, had achieved her dreams and found her place in life.

***

Two hours later, Rupert Gardon was on his way to a luxurious drug rehab center courtesy of his father, his three thug friends were in jail, and Beatrice Gardon and her children were already back home.

Jordan and Eden Montgomery, along with Riley Ingram and Justin Kelly, had headed back to headquarters for new assignments. The rest of the LCR crew, Thorne, Cavanaugh, Angela, and Jake, sat around the table at Luigi's All American Pub and rehashed the events.

"Rupert Gardon shouldn't be in a rehab facility," Cavanaugh said, "The asshole needs to be in jail with his buddies."

Jake agreed. When Gardon's father had asked for LCR's help, he had described the situation as a simple domestic dispute. This had been a million miles past simple. The idiot could have blown up his entire family. Not to mention the LCR operatives who had been trying to save them.

"I heard McCall had a few words with the father," Thorne said.

Yeah. Jake had been in the office when Cavanaugh's request for reinforcements came in. Jake had seen his boss in many different moods but he'd never seen him like that. If Arthur Gardon had been face to face with McCall, the man would be sporting some major bruises. The LCR leader had been livid.

Having just returned from a grueling month-long rescue mission in the States, Jake had been exhausted. His plan was to give McCall a brief report of the successful op and then go looking for Angela. He'd been so tired that the only thing keeping him from keeling over was the need to see her and get everything out in the open. It had been simmering in him for weeks.

Despite his exhaustion, when he'd heard Cavanaugh's request, he had been about to offer his help. Even though he wanted to get the confrontation with Angela over as soon as possible, his duty to LCR overrode his personal needs. The instant he'd learned who one of the operatives in danger was, his offer became something else. Nothing could have stopped him from joining the op.

"Yeah," Jake said. "I don't think Gardon will be calling on LCR again."

"So what went down inside?" Angela said.

Thorne, who usually had a semi-pleasant expression on his face, looked pissed as he said, "When we got inside, we were greeted by Rupert's friends. They were all wearing the same outfit—AK-47s."

"It's a wonder they didn't shoot you as soon as they saw you," Angela said.

Thorne grinned, his grim expression replaced with his usual humor. "Yeah, well, just cause the idiots had the weapons didn't mean they knew how to use them. We got two of them disarmed quick." The grin disappeared as he added. "The other one got off a few rounds before we could neutralize him. That's when Gardon forced his wife out of the house."

And Jake would never forget what happened next. Seeing Angela in that kind of danger was the stuff of nightmares. But damn if she hadn't handled herself like a pro.

He'd had a month to think about what he'd done and now, nothing was going to stop him from saying what he needed to say. Problem was, did she want to hear it? Other than her initial "What are you doing here?" Angela hadn't spoken to him, had barely even looked at him. Was he too late? Had he fucked it up so bad, he couldn't fix it?

No, he refused to believe that. She'd damn well listen to him…she had to.

Cavanaugh took a long swallow from his beer and stood. "I'm headed to my room for some shuteye. The plane leaves at 0700." He shot a glance at Thorne. "You coming?"

His gaze going from Jake to Angela, he slumped back in his chair with a lazy grin. "Nah. Think I'll stay a while longer."

The grin turned to a painful grimace when Cavanaugh's hand landed hard on the man's shoulder. "Let's go, Thorne."

Jake threw Cavanaugh a grateful smile while Thorne winked at them both and got up. "Come to think of it, I am kind of sleepy."

The two men disappeared out the door, leaving Jake and Angela alone at last. Unsure how to start, he cleared his throat. He'd never been one for declarations so damned if he could figure out the exact words he wanted to say, especially about something this important. After having had weeks to think about it, one would think he'd have a whole speech prepared. But instead of spilling his guts, he heard himself say, "How are you feeling?"

"Good. Completely fit. I think the scars on my feet will completely fade with time."

"That's good."

Hell, he felt like he had sawdust in his mouth. Swallowing, he was about to say something hopefully meaningful when she gave him unexpected news.

"Delacourte's dead."

"What happened?"

"Someone got to him in jail. The theory is that a relative of one of the victims paid to have him killed."

"The world's a better place without him."

"I agree." She looked down at her hands, a clear indication that she was uncomfortable.

Jake cleared his throat. "Can we go somewhere and talk privately?"

She looked around. "This isn't private?"

"Not the kind I'm going to need."

"I see." She grabbed her purse and slid off her stool. "We can go to my hotel room."

Angela watched as Jake shoved his chair back and threw money down for their tab. Why was he here? The moment she had seen him, all she could think about was throwing herself into his arms. If Beatrice Gardon hadn't had dynamite strapped to her body, that's exactly what she would have done.

Was he going to try to talk her out of being an operative again? She was tired and vulnerable tonight. If he asked, she wasn't sure she wouldn't at least tell him she would think about it just to have him hold her again. Angela hated that she was so weak but it had always been that way with Jake. She wanted to please him.

They walked the short distance to the hotel in silence. It was past one in the morning and only a few people were around. She breathed in the fragrance of the spring night and tried to pretend, for just a moment, that all was right in her world. That she and Jake had just come off a successful mission and were enjoying some downtime together.

The fantasy lasted until they walked into her room. Then the silence, instead of easy and comfortable, became painful. Angela moved across the room to the window and leaned against it, her arms crossed. As much as she wanted to say things to make it all better, she couldn't. And if she stayed close to him, she knew she wouldn't be able to resist touching him.

Jake sat on the edge of the bed and faced her. "I've missed you."

"I've missed you, too."

"I've had a lot of time to think about things."

Angela tensed. The expression on his face was impossible to read.

"I came back here to ask you to reconsider being an operative."

Her heart plunged and despair filled her again. Angela opened her mouth to once again try to convince him to change his mind when he added, "And then when I saw how you handled yourself today, I realized I couldn't. You were in your element, doing what you've always wanted to do and doing a damn good job." He shook his head. "I should never have asked you to give up your dreams."

Hope rising, her voice was so thick she hardly recognized it as hers. "So what are you saying?"

"I'm saying that…" He stopped and shoved his fingers through his hair. "I'm saying that whether you're an LCR operative, a researcher or hell, a stripper, I don't care."

She'd gone from hopeless to ecstatic and now she was somewhere in limbo, being tortured by uncertainty. What was he trying to tell her?

"What, Jake?"

A faraway look came over his face. "When Teresa was killed, I spent a lot of time thinking about all the things I didn't get to say to her, all the things I wished we had done together. All the time we wasted that we didn't even realize was a waste."

Still not breathing, Angela waited.

Blue eyes glinting with more emotion than she'd ever seen in them, Jake continued, "Bottom line—I don't want to live without you. I've wasted enough time as it is. So if it's only a day, a month, or a year that I can be with you, I don't want to miss another minute of it."

She held on to the windowsill behind her to keep from running across the room, into his arms. "What happens when I'm on an op? How are you going to handle it?"

"I won't lie to you…I'll worry. I hope to be with you on most of them but if I can't be, I trust you to know how to handle yourself."

Angela leaped toward him and Jake caught her, swinging her around in his arms. Then setting her feet on the floor, he cupped her face in his hands. "You're the most amazing woman I've ever known, Angela Delvecchio. I want to spend the rest of my life with you."

She stood on her toes to kiss him and was surprised when he pulled away. "What's wrong?"

"I have something to show you." He backed up and unbuttoned his shirt. So mesmerized by the beautiful muscled chest he was revealing, she missed his next words.

"What?" she asked.

"It's a message for you." Shrugging his shirt off, he dropped it to the floor and turned his back to her.

Something was written on the back of his neck. She drew closer and her eyes filled with tears. In the exact place where she had her rose tattoo with the word 'survivor' in the middle, he'd had tattooed on his neck: *I love a survivor.*

Swallowing a sob of joy, Angela leaped at him again. He turned at the last second, caught her in his arms and then fell onto the bed with her beside him. Covering her face with kisses, he licked at the salty tears streaming down her face.

"I thought you hated needles," she said breathlessly.

"I do, but you, Angela Delvecchio, I adore."

"And I love and adore you, Jake Mallory."

"Partners at work and at home?"

"Yes, partners," she whispered.

"Forever?"

Her heart soaring, she spoke against his mouth, "Forever."

# EPILOGUE

*Three Months Later*

*The McCall's house*

*Paris*

"You think they'll be surprised or upset?"

Lifting a strand of Mara's silky black hair, Noah pushed it aside to reveal a bare, elegant shoulder. Bending down, he pressed a kiss to her creamy skin, breathed in her subtle delicate perfume and wished they had time for more. With guests numbering close to a hundred arriving in a matter of minutes, he knew that wasn't possible.

With a sigh of regret, he backed away and then noticed the worried wrinkle above the bridge of her nose. This decision hadn't been easy for either of them.

"A few will be surprised. The ones who know us best probably won't be. No one's going to be angry but yeah, a few of them will be upset."

"It's going to be hard to say goodbye."

"We'll still see them."

"I know, but they've been my family since I moved here."

Noah drew in a settling breath. He was doing his best not to think about that part of his decision. Last Chance Rescue had started in Paris with nothing more than a dream, determination, sweat, and the occasional bloodletting. Saying goodbye would be like losing a limb.

Still, he knew this was for the best. Taking his wife into his arms, he held her tight. How he'd been so blessed was still a mystery to him. And he was going to do whatever it took to keep his Mara happy.

"Micah and Evie need to be close to their grandparents. And they're missing out on having dozens of cousins, not to mention aunts and uncles doting on them."

Five years ago, he would've laughed his ass off if anyone had told him he'd actually move thousands of miles and interrupt his entire operation to be close to a large family. But for Mara and his children? He would move the earth itself if he could. There was nothing he wouldn't do for them.

Pulling away from him with a sniff, she asked, "Have I mentioned lately that you're the most wonderful man in the world?"

He smiled down at the woman who was his heart…his life. "Not in the last couple of hours."

The doorbell chimed, telling them their first guests had arrived.

Samara stood on her toes and whispered in his ear, "Be prepared to hear it several times tonight."

His heart clenching with emotion, the smile disappeared from his face.

"What's wrong?" Samara asked.

"Just thinking how much I love you."

Giving him the hot, wicked look that always sent his body pulsing with need, she winked. "That's something you can tell me several times tonight, too."

"Deal." He kissed her hand, then engulfed it in his larger one and pulled her with him to the door. No matter where they lived, as long as he had Mara and his children, he would be a happy man.

And LCR would continue to thrive. He already had plans in place. If things worked out the way he wanted, the organization that had started with two clueless men and a dream would expand beyond their wildest expectations.

The door opened and Angela beamed at Noah and Samara. Lately, her mouth couldn't seem to stop smiling. This was the first social event she and Jake had attended as a couple. Silly, but she was nervous. Even though she and Jake had been together for several months, they had yet to make any kind of announcement about their relationship.

Noah had partnered them on several missions and though they still had a few kinks to work out, things had gone even better than she could have hoped. Having Jake as her partner at work and at home was her dream come true.

And now they were telling the world that their partnership extended beyond work. An LCR social event was a rarity of its own. Appearing together as a couple was definitely a public statement of intent.

As Samara hugged her and then took her purse, Angela asked, "Are we too early?"

"Of course not. You're right on time."

Angela took note of her friend's glistening eyes. Something was going on. The couple of times she'd seen Noah this week, he had been quiet and pensive. A familiar fear tugged at her heart. She hated to be a pessimist but now that things were so wonderful for her and Jake, she couldn't help but fear that something would happen to one of her loved ones to spoil her happiness.

They went into the large, beautifully decorated living room. Samara's taste ran from bold to peaceful, splashes of bright colors blended beautifully with serene pastels. Looking around for the two dark-haired little imps she adored, Angela said, "Where are Micah and Evie?"

"They're staying the night with Candace," Samara said.

Candace was the children's part-time nanny. "I didn't know they stayed overnight yet."

"They don't. This is their first time." She grinned and added, "Micah was ecstatic, looking at it as a big adventure. Evie wasn't happy at all. I don't know who cried the most when they left, me or Evie."

"Then why—"

"We just thought it would be best if they were out of the house tonight."

Before she could ask why, the doorbell rang. While Noah went to answer the door, Samara excused herself to check something in the kitchen. Angela turned to Jake. "Something's going on."

"Yeah, I agree. I'm sure they'll tell us when they're ready." He leaned down and kissed her forehead. "Did I tell you how beautiful you look tonight?"

She laughed and could feel a blush heat her face. "Actually you did. Twice. That's why I thought we would be late."

The look on his face could only be called smug. Angela had been dressed and ready to go but when Jake had seen the black backless dress she was wearing, he had insisted she take it off so he could help her back on with it. Things had gotten beautifully out of hand and she had enjoyed every moment.

"You keep looking at me like that and I'll have to take that dress off of you again."

The sexy growl in her ear sent shivers of delight zipping up her spine. "I'll look forward to that." She looked him up and down. "Did I happen to mention how good you look?"

"Yeah." He leaned closer and murmured, "I think I was inside you at the time."

She laughed and lightly punched his shoulder. "Behave. And for the record, I didn't say you looked good at that particular time."

Blue eyes twinkled with devilment. "No? But you screamed, "So good!" at the top of your lungs. I thought that's what you meant."

Smiling and blushing once more, Angela shook her head. When it came to sexual repartee, Jake was a master.

"Looks like it's going to be a full house tonight."

She turned to see Jordan and Eden coming into the room, followed by Honor and Seth. Behind the Cavanaughs were Ethan and Shea Bishop, McKenna and Lucas Kane, and Jamie and Dylan Savage. She gasped in surprise when she saw Gabe and Skylar Maddox, and then behind them were Cole and Keeley Mathison. What on earth was going on here?

As she went about hugging everyone, Angela put aside her worry and set out to enjoy herself. Something was on the horizon, that was for sure. But with Jake at her side—her lover, her partner, her friend—whatever winds of change came her way, she knew everything would be just fine.

**Thank you for reading *Chances Are*! I hope you enjoyed it. If you did, please help other readers find this book:**

1. This book is lendable. Share it with a friend who would enjoy a dark and steamy romantic suspense and introduce them to the Last Chance Rescue series.
2. Help other people find this book by writing a review.
3. Sign up for my newsletter at *http://christyreece.com* to learn about upcoming books.
4. Come like my Facebook page at *https://www.facebook.com/AuthorChistyReece*
5. Come like my Last Chance Rescue Facebook page for exclusive book excerpts at *https://www.facebook.com/LastChanceRescuebooksbychristyreece*

# ACKNOWLEDGEMENTS:

Special thanks to the following people for helping make this book possible:

My wonderful husband for his incredible support, gifts of chocolate, and many moments of comic relief.

My friend and fabulous author Marie Force, for her help, encouragement, and wonderful advice. And to her eBook Formatting Fairies who answered my endless questions with endless patience.

My first readers, Anne, Crystal, Jackie, and Kara, who read several versions of this book and were phenomenally helpful.

And an extra special thank you to my readers. Without you, this book and all the others, past and future, would not be possible. You make my dreams come true!

# ABOUT THE AUTHOR

Christy Reece is the award winning and NYT Bestselling author of dark and sexy romantic suspense. She lives in Alabama with her husband, four precocious fur-kids, and a very shy turtle. You can contact her at *Christy@christyreece.com*

Christy also writes Steamy, Southern Suspense under the pen name Ella Grace. *http://ellagracebooks.com*

Praise for Christy Reece and her novels:

"The type of book you will pick up and NEVER want to put down again." *Coffee Time Romance and More*

"Romantic suspense has a major new star!" *Romantic Times Magazine*

"Sizzling romance and fraught suspense fill the pages as the novel races toward its intensely riveting conclusion." *Publishers Weekly, Starred Review*

"Flat-out scary, and I loved every minute of it!" *The Romance Reader's Connection*

"A brilliantly plotted book. Her main characters are vulnerable yet strong, and even the villains are written with skillful and delicate brush strokes haunting your mind long after the book is done." *Fresh Fiction*

"A passionate and vivacious thrill-ride! … I feel like I've been on an epic journey after finishing it.... Exquisite." *Joyfully Reviewed*

Turn the page to read an exclusive teaser from

RUNNING ON EMPTY

the next novel in Christy Reece's Last Chance Rescue series!

# CHAPTER ONE

Los Rios, Mexico

The dance was on.

LCR operative Sabrina Fox lifted her long, auburn hair and with a twist of her wrist, expertly created a sexy, elegant up-do. Her game face was officially in place. Looking in the mirror was a little like watching a familiar play. She knew the cast, the script, and the lines she would deliver. The only question was how the other cast members would respond. Fortunately she was prepared for every possible scenario. And like any good actress, she knew when to make her exit.

Once the play ended, she would go back to being Sabrina. Tonight she was Lucia St. Andre, auditioning to be the mistress of a cold-hearted, sadistic bastard named Reuben Pierce.

Not that a real audition would take place. She had lured more than one man with promises of ecstasy and left him waiting, wanting…and occasionally in the hospital. She had played this scenario out only a couple of times as an operative for Last Chance Rescue. In her previous job, acting the femme fatale had been her primary role. She was glad to finally have some diversity.

A soft chime alerted her it was show time. Sabrina turned away from the mirror and exited her room without a backward glance. Her black evening gown was both elegant and understated. She would be accepted in any high society dinner party and would likely be the most conservatively dressed woman in attendance.

There was no reason to flaunt her body. The man she was here to entice could have her stripped with one look. Not that she planned to allow that, but advertising her body wasn't her intent. Mystery and allure would hook the man, not blatant sexuality. With Reuben Pierce's money and influence, he could have some of the most beautiful women in the world at his beck and call. Though Sabrina knew she was attractive, she was no great beauty. What she lacked in looks, she made up for in many other ways. Talents that would appeal to Reuben.

A tall, gaunt man stood at the entrance to the room where Sabrina had been told to come at the sound of the chime. Slightly bugged eyes dragged down her body and then he gave what sounded like a disapproving sniff. Extending his wrinkled, scrawny neck only slightly, the man intoned in a pretentious and laughably fake British accent, "Mr. Pierce will see you now."

The Igor-like man pushed the door open and Sabrina stepped into another world.

20070198R00134

Made in the USA
San Bernardino, CA
26 March 2015